He needed to h

He wasn't in the best of moods, but she had to tell him. She had to tell him now while there was still time.…

"I have something to tell you, Nick." She stood up even though her knees were shaking as much as her voice.

"You're trembling like a leaf," Nick said softly, then gently settled her on the sofa. He squatted down beside her, bringing his blue eyes level with hers.

This revelation was going to be difficult. She drew a deep breath and closed her eyes. She opened her mouth to reveal the one thing her husband didn't want to hear.

"Nick, I'm pregnant.…"

Dear Reader,

Spring cleaning wearing you out? Perk up with a heart-thumping romance from Silhouette Romance. This month, your favorite authors return to the line, and a new one makes her debut!

Take a much-deserved break with bestselling author Judy Christenberry's secret-baby story, *Daddy on the Doorstep* (#1654). Then plunge into Elizabeth August's latest, *The Rancher's Hand-Picked Bride* (#1656), about a celibate heroine forced to find her rugged neighbor a bride!

You won't want to miss the first in Raye Morgan's CATCHING THE CROWN miniseries about three royal siblings raised in America who must return to their kingdom and marry. In *Jack and the Princess* (#1655), Princess Karina falls for her bodyguard, but what will it take for this gruff commoner to win a place in the royal family? And in Diane Pershing's *The Wish* (#1657), the next SOULMATES installment, a pair of magic eyeglasses gives Gerri Conklin the chance to do over the most disastrous week of her life...and find the man of her dreams!

And be sure to keep your eye on these two Romance authors. Roxann Delaney delivers her third fabulous Silhouette Romance novel, *A Whole New Man* (#1658), about a live-for-the-moment hero transformed into a family man, but will it last? And Cheryl Kushner makes her debut with *He's Still the One* (#1659), a fresh, funny, heartwarming tale about a TV show host who returns to her hometown and the man she never stopped loving.

Happy reading!

Mary-Theresa Hussey

Mary-Theresa Hussey
Senior Editor

Please address questions and book requests to:
Silhouette Reader Service
U.S.: 3010 Walden Ave., P.O. Box 1325, Buffalo, NY 14269
Canadian: P.O. Box 609, Fort Erie, Ont. L2A 5X3

Daddy on
the Doorstep

JUDY CHRISTENBERRY

SILHOUETTE *Romance*®

Published by Silhouette Books

America's Publisher of Contemporary Romance

SILHOUETTE BOOKS

ISBN 0-373-19654-7

DADDY ON THE DOORSTEP

This edition published by arrangement with Harlequin Books S.A.

® and TM are trademarks of Harlequin Books S.A., used under license. Trademarks indicated with ® are registered in the United States Patent and Trademark Office, the Canadian Trade Marks Office and in other countries.

Visit Silhouette at www.eHarlequin.com

Printed in U.S.A.

JUDY CHRISTENBERRY

has been writing romances for over fifteen years because she loves happy endings as much as her readers do. She's also a bestselling author for Harlequin American Romance, but she has a long love of traditional romances and is delighted to tell a story that brings those elements to the reader. A former high school French teacher, Judy devotes her time to writing. She hopes readers have as much fun reading her stories as she does writing them. She spends her spare time reading, watching her favorite sports teams and keeping track of her two adult daughters.

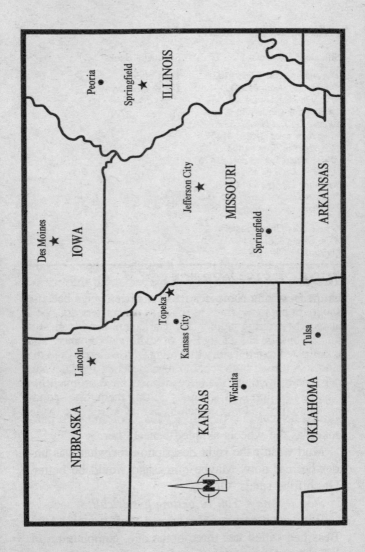

Chapter One

Andrea Bainbridge peered through the sheets of rain deluging her windshield and prayed she'd make it to Aunt Bess's house before her car was swept off the road. She could barely see the pavement. Only the center white line kept her on track.

Afraid to go above a snail's pace, Andrea thought she'd never reach the long drive that led to Aunt Bess's farmhouse. When she finally saw the outline of the familiar mailbox through the pouring rain, she turned her car into the drive with relief and then panicked as the wheels skidded beneath her.

Mud wasn't the right description for what was under her car now. Maybe quicksand would be better. Or shifting sands. Or—

Stop it, Andy! You're getting hysterical!

With good reason, she argued with herself. Aunt Bess had called her three hours ago, complaining of chest pains. Andrea hadn't been able to convince the stubborn old lady to go to the hospital without her. Bess had assured her she could wait until Andrea arrived.

Normally she could make the drive in a little less than two hours. But these conditions weren't normal. It had been raining day and night for almost a month. Andrea knew how Noah had felt. All the rivers and streams had flooded days ago. There was only one road to Bess's farm which was still above water.

And she wasn't sure how much longer it would be open. She'd been petrified when she'd crossed that one-lane wooden bridge.

The car slid out of control and she fought the steering wheel. When she finally came to a halt, she was almost sideways in the small lane.

"Hold on, Bess. I'm coming," she muttered, more for herself than Bess. But the old lady was the one person in this world Andrea loved without reservation. She'd do anything for Aunt Bess.

Carefully backing up, she braked and then put the car in Drive. The tires spun and she swallowed her fear. Easing off the gas pedal, she allowed the forward motion of the gear to move the car. Once the tires had gripped whatever solid ground there was, she pressed slightly on the pedal and breathed a sigh of relief as the car moved forward.

When the dim form of the old farmhouse became visible, Andrea killed the motor and leaped from the car. She wasn't worried about the rain or the mud, only about Bess. She had to get her to a hospital.

"Bess? Bess?" she called as she swung open the front door.

Silence greeted her. Fearing what she might find, Andrea raced to the kitchen, the true center of Aunt Bess's home, but it was empty.

From there, she ran to the bedroom. More silence.

"Bess? Where are you?" Panic rising, she raced back through to the living room and the front door. That's when she saw the message taped to the panel of glass.

Andy,

I persuaded Bess to let me take her to the hospital before you got here. I didn't think she should wait. Hope I did the right thing.

Roy Evans

Andrea slumped against the door, relieved beyond words that Bess was in good hands. Roy Evans was a nearby neighbor who checked on Bess almost every day. Then, concern about Roy's statement about not waiting filled Andrea and she ran back to the kitchen and the phone on the wall.

Bess kept her telephone directory on a shelf below the phone and Andrea thumbed through it impatiently, searching for the number to the small hospital in the closest town. As she was dialing the number, concentrating on Bess's safety with all her heart, she vaguely heard more noise, though it was hard to detect a difference over the roar of the storm.

"Hubbard Hospital," a clipped voice answered and

then spoke to someone else before Andrea could ask about Bess. "No, sir, you can't go back there. You're getting in the doctor's way!"

"Please," Andrea interrupted, "I need to find out about—"

"Hello? Hello? Is anyone here?"

Andrea stared at the phone receiver briefly before she realized this new voice wasn't coming over the wire. It was coming from the front door.

And she recogized the voice. It belonged to her soon-to-be ex-husband, Nicholas Avery.

She hung up the phone and hurried to the front of the house, unable to believe her ears. Nick, the last she'd heard, had been missing after he'd gone to Africa on a business trip.

"Aunt Bess?" he called.

"Nick?" she questioned even as her eyes confirmed her earlier guess. "What are you doing here?"

Okay, she hadn't sounded welcoming, but what did he expect? There was no need for him to frown at her like that.

"I think that's my line, isn't it, Andy? After all, Bess is my aunt."

"But you were missing—"

"And now I'm found. Where's Aunt Bess?" he snapped.

"At…at the hospital, I think." His question had made her remember the important person in their little drama. "She left a note. Her neighbor took her to the hospital."

"She's hurt?" he asked, urgency in his voice.

"She called me earlier. Told me she was having chest pains and wouldn't go to the doctor until I came."

"A heart attack?" Nick asked with even more urgency. She'd never seen her husband lose his cool. Ex-husband, she corrected herself. Or soon to be. But he seemed close to the edge now. That was one thing they'd always had in common. They both loved Bess.

"I was calling the hospital when I heard you. I'll call again." This time she asked her question as soon as the operator answered.

"I'll ring her room, but make your call brief. We've got a lot of emergencies and we need to keep the lines open."

"Aunt Bess," Andrea said in relief when a quavery voice answered.

"Is that you, Andy? Thank God. I was so worried. Where are you?"

Andrea didn't get a chance to answer. Nick took the phone from her hand.

"Aunt Bess? It's Nick. I'm home. Are you okay?"

Bess was his aunt, his mother's sister, so she guessed Nick technically had the right to be the one to talk to her. And she knew Bess would be relieved. She'd called Andrea almost a week ago to tell her Nick had flown to Africa on business and then disappeared. The State Department had been unable to offer any information about his safety.

She'd talked to Bess each evening, the two of them sharing their fears. That's why Nick's appearance had been even more of a surprise than normal.

"Is she all right?" Andrea asked impatiently, watching his face.

Ignoring her question, he continued to talk to his aunt. "Yes, I will. Take care of yourself."

He replaced the receiver without offering it to Andrea.

"I wanted to talk to her!" she exclaimed, frustration rising.

"The operator cut in and asked us to hang up. Aunt Bess is okay. The doctor thinks it was indigestion."

"Indigestion?" she questioned faintly. Indigestion. She'd worried herself sick, driven through a major storm, and unexpectedly had to face Nick. All for indigestion.

And she'd do the same thing again. She wouldn't take any chances with Bess's health. "I'm glad," she whispered.

Nick made no response, only stared at her. Chilled by the coldness in his eyes, she stepped around him and headed for the front door.

"Where are you going?"

"To the hospital." She didn't expect him to ask her to stay. He probably didn't want to talk to her any more than she wanted to talk to him. However, he surprised her by catching her arm.

"No, you're not."

"What are you talking about?" she protested. "Of course I am. Let me go!"

"Andy! Listen to me. The bridge is out."

"Nice try. I just crossed over that bridge." And she dreaded the thought of doing so again.

"I flew in on the police helicoptor. We watched it wash away."

The sincerity in his voice almost convinced her. But she couldn't face the prospect of staying here alone with him. "I don't believe you," she insisted, and turned back toward the door.

He wouldn't let her go. "Andy. Use your head for once. You can't go!"

She wrenched her coat from his hold. "Use my head for once?" she repeated, glaring at him. Then she snapped her mouth shut and ran to the front door.

He called her name above the storm and she was sure he pursued her. Nick never gave in or admitted he'd been bested. But this time she would do things her way. Tumbling down the steps into the rain, she had to slow down or she'd lose her footing. Too bad she left the car so far from the porch. But she'd been in as big a hurry when she'd arrived, as she was now.

He caught her just as she rounded the front of the car. She turned to scream at him over the thunder and rain. Before she could say anything, however, he yanked her toward him and they both fell into the mud. Even as she raised up to ask him if he was crazy, a louder noise stunned her.

She looked up at a roof of sodden greenness. And a deep crease in the roof of her car. A nearby tree, its roots exposed by the washing away of the soil the past month, had been blown across her car.

Another foot and that crease would have been in her head. She'd have been dead. If Nick hadn't stopped her, that tree would have fallen on her.

Stunned by that cataclysmic thought, Andrea turned to stare at him. He was rising to his feet, without letting go of her, his clothing covered in mud, rain streaming down him. For the first time, she realized she was in much the same condition.

"Andy, are you hurt?" he gently demanded as he slid his hands beneath her arms to lift her.

"No—no, I don't think so." Trembling seized her, but whether it was from the cold or the shock, she didn't know.

"Come on, we've got to get inside and get warm and dry. Can you walk?"

He didn't wait for her to answer. As efficient as always, he led her to the porch. "Take off your clothes."

Had he lost his mind? She stared at him, wondering if she was having a nightmare.

"Andy," he explained, his voice laden with exasperation, "you're wet and muddy. There's no point in dragging these clothes through the house. Take them off and go get in the shower."

The thought of a hot shower was heavenly; stripping in front of Nick was not. Even if what he said made sense, she wasn't prepared to make herself so vulnerable to him. "Turn around."

"Andy, you're being ridiculous!" he exploded.

She raised her chin and stared at him, but her rebellion was undermined by the shivering that seized her.

"Damn, you're a stubborn woman!"

Before she could decide her next step, he abruptly spun around, turning his back to her.

It took her a second to realize he was complying with her request. Then she hurriedly started removing the wet, muddy clothes. As she reached her underwear, her shivering became almost uncontrollable.

"Haven't you finished yet?" Nick demanded.

"Yes. I'm going in now."

"Don't use all the hot water," he shouted after her.

She raced to the only bathroom, next to Bess's bedroom, and slammed the door behind her. Quickly removing her underwear, she stepped beneath the hot spray of the shower. It took several minutes for her skin to respond, but gradually the chill disappeared.

A loud banging on the door almost caused her to lose her footing. "Andy? Here's your bag. And hurry. I'm half frozen." The bathroom door opened and closed.

She turned off the water and pulled back the curtain. Her suitcase sat on the bathroom mat. Quickly she dried off and dug into the bag. In only minutes she opened the bathroom door to discover Nick leaning against the bedroom wall, his bareness minimally covered by a bath towel. She couldn't hold back a gasp as her gaze encountered his broad chest.

Her mouth dry, she moved away from the bathroom door and gestured for him to enter. Words were beyond her.

"Thanks. By the way, I didn't bring any clothes with me. Unless you want me to wear a towel until we can get out of here, see what you can find for me to put on." He ignored her gaping mouth and closed the bathroom door behind him.

Andrea gulped. Did she want him to wear a bath towel until they were rescued? The man was insane. As she would be if she were constantly exposed to that much of Nick's well-muscled, tempting skin.

The sound of the shower awoke her from her stupor, and she headed for the basement door. The last time she'd spent a weekend with Bess, she'd been sorting old clothes. If she hadn't yet given them to charity, surely there would be something for Nick to wear. There had to be.

She returned to the bedroom just as the shower shut off.

"Nick?" she called through the closed door.

"Yeah?"

"I've found a few things from the basement. I'll toss them in." She hurriedly did what she'd said and pulled the door closed again, as if afraid the steam might escape. As she did so, she heard Nick shove back the shower curtain.

Visions of him stepping from the shower, his dark hair curling from the steam, his body glistening with droplets of water, made her stomach turn over.

She wasn't going to think about it. Her marriage to Nick was over. Those days were behind her. And she was glad. She swallowed the pain she'd been trying to ignore for the past month. Right, she was glad.

Anxious to occupy her mind with something other than Nick, she hurried to the kitchen and put on a kettle of water. She and Bess loved to share their secrets over a cup of hot tea. She didn't want to share any secrets with Nick, but at least making tea gave her something to do.

"Do you think *Gentleman's Quarterly* will want photos?" Nick asked, his voice husky.

Andrea whirled around, one hand going to her throat. He'd sounded just like that when they'd made love, exhorting her to greater heights. Her memories, those forbidden memories, were driven from her head when she got a good look at the tall, virile man striking a ridiculous pose in the doorway.

Though lean and fit, Nick was a big man. At six foot three, he towered over her. He'd also towered over his uncle, now long dead, because the overalls he was wearing ended a good four inches above his feet, enclosed in striped socks. On the other hand, his uncle must have required more room at his waist because the denim material flapped around Nick's middle.

Underneath the straps of the overalls he wore a gray sweatshirt that stopped at his waist and fit his broad chest like a second skin. The sleeves ended above his wrists.

In spite of the trauma of the past few hours, Andrea burst out laughing. *"Très chic!"*

She was reminded of the danger Nick represented when his sexy grin appeared, and he took a step toward her. She quickly backed away.

"Where are you going?"

"Um, I'm fixing some tea. Do you want some?"

Turning her back to him, she opened the box of tea bags just as the kettle began to sing.

"Yeah."

In that one word he let her know that he was no happier about their situation than she was. To avoid looking at him, she busied herself with the mugs and spoons, the cream and sugar, moving it all to the table, then finding a saucer for the oatmeal-raisin cookies Bess always had on hand.

By the time she brought the kettle to the table to pour boiling water into the mugs, Nick had sat down and was waiting. Though it was a cowardly thought, she wished she could come up with a reason to take her tea to another room. But he'd only follow her.

Or would he? He certainly hadn't followed her when she'd left their home, their marriage. He'd apparently accepted her exit with equanimity. And that was what she wanted, she quickly reminded herself. Exactly what she wanted.

"Thanks."

She nodded in return, agreeable to talking in monosyllables. At least that limited their topics of discussion.

"Has it been raining the whole time I was gone?"

He'd left for Africa three weeks ago. The rain had begun almost a week later, but no one had expected it to last so long.

"Just about."

"Things looked pretty bad from the air. Has Aunt Bess had any trouble? She could have contacted my office. My staff was instructed to help with anything she needed."

Andrea sipped her tea and then nibbled on a cookie, studiously counting the raisins as if she were a quality control inspector.

"You've stayed in touch?" he asked.

She stared at him before returning to her contemplation of the cookie. Was he upset that she hadn't turned her back on Aunt Bess? Well, tough.

"Yes."

He heaved a sigh that would've launched a kite. "Andy, could you give me more than one-word sentences?"

Her gaze returned to his and she raised her chin in defiance. Before he could say anything else, however, she gained control of her temper. She would not act like a child. "I beg your pardon. So much has happened, I'm afraid I'm not myself. Yes, of course, I stayed in touch with Aunt Bess. We're friends."

"You also don't have to treat me like a stranger you've just met. We were married, damn it. Still are, for that matter." Though he kept his voice even, his blue eyes were chilly.

She addressed the only thing of importance in his remarks. "I've been intending to apply for a divorce, but—but it's expensive." That was the truth, but it wasn't the only reason. Otherwise she would have taken out a loan. "If you're in a hurry—"

"No."

Risking a brief glance at him through her lashes, she then picked up her spoon and needlessly stirred her tea. Was he angry that she hadn't started proceedings? What was wrong with him? He could divorce *her,* if he was in a hurry.

Her eyes widened at the thought, and she looked at him again. "Have *you* applied for a divorce?"

"No."

She straightened her back. "What was it you said to me? 'Couldn't I talk in more than one word sentences?' The same to you, Nick."

"All right," he drawled, giving her a level stare. "I have no intention of applying for a divorce. If you decide to do so, that is your business."

As if it didn't affect him in any way, she thought resentfully. But then, that had been the problem with their marriage, too. He seemed totally unaffected by it. Except in the bedroom.

She immediately shut down those thoughts. "More tea?" she offered, since she didn't know what else to say.

"No, I don't want any more damn tea!"

"Then perhaps we'd better talk about how we're going to get out of here. It's almost three o'clock. Can you get the helicopter to come back for us?"

"I can try," he said, and rose from the table.

Try? The great Nicholas Avery never failed. He was the wonder of the financial world, a touchstone of success that had everyone crowding around him. If he wanted the helicopter to come back, it would come back. Even if he had to buy it.

"We're out of luck," he said seconds later, turning back to the table.

"What are you talking about? Are they too busy? Will they come later?"

"I have no idea. The phone is dead."

Chapter Two

"What?" Andrea exclaimed. She jumped to her feet and hurried to the telephone.

When she lifted the receiver, Nick growled, "Can't you even believe me about the stupid phone?"

Her cheeks flushed red, Andrea looked away from Nick as she hung up the receiver. They had never argued while they were married until the night before Andrea had decided to leave him. Then, as now, she'd expressed disbelief at something Nick had said.

"I just—it was a natural reaction," she assured him and then hurriedly asked, "do you think they'll fix it anytime soon?"

As if nature wanted to answer her question, a loud boom of thunder shook the house.

Nick gave her a sardonic grin. "Anything else you want to know?"

She gritted her teeth. "Yes. What are we going to do?"

"Stay inside where it's dry. We should be all right. Aunt Bess could feed an army at a moment's notice. Even if the electricity goes off; we've got—"

"Do you think it will?" Andrea asked with a gasp, nervously looking at the overhead light.

"Andy, relax. If it does, we have oil lamps and firewood. No problem."

His casual dismissal of their predicament irritated her. He'd accused her of overreacting when they'd argued. She hadn't liked it then and she hated it now.

"Fine," she snapped, and turned her back on him, crossing her arms over her chest. No problem? Even with all the electricity she wanted, she'd still be stuck here alone with Nick. If that wasn't a problem, she didn't know what was.

Feeling his stare on her, she whirled back around. "I'm going to find something to read," she muttered without looking at him. Bess was a prolific reader and kept a lot of books around the house. Andrea needed something to take her mind off the six-foot-three bundle of trouble staring at her.

"I think I'll take a nap, if you don't need me," Nick offered in return. "I'm still on Africa time."

She risked a look and immediately noted the shadows under his eyes. Why hadn't she seen them before? Probably because she'd been distracted by his body, she admitted to herself. And because she was afraid to look him in the eye for any length of time.

Those eyes of his could mesmerize her faster than a rattler could lure an innocent rabbit to come closer.

"Fine," she agreed, and entered the living room to search for a book.

Something was pulling her from sleep. Andrea shifted and banged her elbow into hardness. Funny, she thought fuzzily, what's the wall doing there? Her bed wasn't next to the wall.

Even as that thought came, she noticed the cut-velvet texture under her cheek and her eyes opened. Aunt Bess. She was at Aunt Bess's house. And Aunt Bess was in the hospital and Nick was here.

With her.

She groaned and sat up, dislodging the book she'd been reading. Not that it had held her interest. She'd checked on Nick several times, enjoying the opportunity to watch him sleep, forbidden fruit as it were.

The urge to join him on the big bed had sent her scurrying back to the sofa in the living room. And her own eventual nap. She was so tired lately.

The deep shadows in the room caught her attention. Had the electricity gone off, as Nick had predicted? She quickly reached for the lamp and breathed a sigh of relief when it clicked on, sending shafts of light around the room.

Her watch read ten past seven, which explained the growl from her stomach. She got up and tiptoed to Bess's bedroom. Pushing the door open only enough to peek in, she discovered Nick was still sleeping. Quietly, she retreated to the kitchen.

Though she was unsure whether Nick would join her for dinner or not, Andrea had no intention of being a martyr and skipping the meal. As Nick had said, Aunt Bess always had more than enough food on hand. After a quick survey, Andrea opened a can of soup and put it on to heat while she fixed some sandwiches from the fresh turkey she found in the refrigerator.

When everything was ready, she went back to the bedroom and pushed the door open slightly again. When it abruptly swung all the way back, she smothered a scream and jumped.

"Easy, there. I didn't mean to scare you," Nick said, though his look wasn't an apology.

"I thought you were still sleeping."

"Were you going to wake me?"

"I don't know. I fixed something to eat, but I didn't know if…if you were hungry." She backed toward the kitchen, unsure what to do next.

"I'm starving," he assured her, his gaze pinned on her face.

"It's only soup and sandwiches."

"Good enough."

He took a step toward her and she turned and fled to the kitchen. Somehow she feared he might mistake her for his meal.

They ate in silence until Nick had finished.

"You've got a healthy appetite," he observed.

Her head snapped up and she stared at him before looking away. "I always have," she said mildly.

"True. But you didn't always look like a waif with

eyes too big for your face. What have you been doing to yourself?''

He continued to stare at her, and the turkey in her mouth tasted like sawdust. She swallowed before replying, ''I've been busy.''

''Too busy to eat?'' he asked skeptically. ''Everyone should make time for proper meals.''

Since he'd constantly missed dinner because of work, Andrea couldn't believe her ears. ''Is this the same man who called most evenings to say he'd grab a bite somewhere, that I shouldn't count on him for dinner?''

He gave her a lopsided grin, almost an apology if she could believe her eyes. ''Maybe I learned the importance of meals after what I had to eat in Africa.''

The reminder of how close she'd come to living in a world without him pierced her heart. She'd accepted that he wasn't going to be a part of her life, but she couldn't bear to think of him dead.

''Was it very bad?''

A low grumble was his first response. When she continued to watch him, he muttered, ''Yeah. Eat your sandwich. You can't afford to waste any calories.''

''Will you tell me about it?'' It would be torture to hear what he'd suffered, but somehow she had to know.

''No. There's no point in talking about it. Eat.''

She shouldn't have been surprised. He hadn't wanted to talk during their marriage. His only interest had been in the bedroom. In the beginning, she'd been so swept off her feet, so overwhelmed by his magneticism, she hadn't noticed how limited their relationship was.

Then he'd taken her to a company dinner. The stunning blonde who worked in accounting discussed business with him. Then they talked about sports, mostly the Chicago Bears. Two men joined them and expanded the conversation to hunting.

Andrea had stood there, realizing for the first time that she had no knowledge of Nick's real life. She could tell the blonde what turned her husband on. She could share with the gentlemen what he said when he reached satisfaction. She knew what he liked her to wear.

But she didn't know him.

They'd only been married a month, after a whirlwind courtship that was even shorter. Andrea set out to correct the difficulty. And found herself blocked at every turn. If she made plans for the two of them, Nick inevitably canceled. Work was too hectic; candlelit dinners ended with her eating alone.

Attempts at conversation either were dismissed because he was too tired...or because he wanted her. When she protested her loneliness, he offered her a bigger allowance and told her to join some clubs.

Most painful of all, when she'd asked about starting a family, he'd flatly refused.

"You're not eating," he reminded her, dragging her from her distasteful memories.

She abruptly stood. "I've finished." Crossing to the sink, she dumped what was left of her sandwich in the trash and began rinsing the dishes. The kitchen was completely up-to-date, thanks to Nick. He couldn't persuade Aunt Bess to move to Chicago, or to let him build her a new house. But she was terribly proud of her new kitchen.

"So, where are you living now?" Nick asked as he sat slouched at the table.

Andrea eyed his casual air, but she wasn't fooled. "You already know."

He didn't move, but his gaze intensified. "What makes you think that?"

"Who else would deposit ten thousand dollars into my checking account?" When she'd gotten the deposit slip in the mail, she'd first thought the bank had made a mistake. But when she'd called, the bank officer had kindly explained that her husband had thought she might need additional funds in her separate account. He even assured her that if she needed more, any check she wrote would be covered by her husband's bank in Chicago.

"I thought you might be strapped for cash. You didn't take much with you." He didn't meet her gaze.

"I'm fine. I can return the money to you whenever you want it." She might not be living in the lap of luxury, but she was managing.

"I don't want the damn money," he replied, straightening, his shoulders stiff.

Forcing herself to remain calm, she crossed to the table and reached for his dishes. In a flash he had seized her wrists, forcing her to stand still.

"Andy, why did you leave?"

Her heart beat faster as she debated her response. They'd had an argument, but she hadn't decided to leave until after he'd left their penthouse, bound for the airport for another business trip. Like most runaways, she'd left a note.

"I—I told you in the note."

"'Our marriage isn't working'? You think that's an explanation for walking out? Hell, we were only married for six months!" His brows furrowed across his forehead and those devilish blue eyes glinted with fury.

She pulled from his grasp. "What do you care? You didn't come after me or call me. You just went on about your business, leader of free enterprise, billionaire extraordinaire."

He rose and Andrea took a step back. "Is that what your leaving was all about? You wanted me to come after you? To prove that I love you? Didn't I tell you I love you? Can't you accept my word? Do I have to—"

"No!" she replied sharply, interrupting his tirade. "No, that wasn't what I wanted. I want a divorce. That's all I want. You can keep your money."

She turned her back to him and took a deep breath, hoping to steady her racing pulse. She needed to stay calm.

When he spoke again, his voice was even, as if he, too, recognized the need for control. "At the moment, you're still my wife, Andy. I'm supposed to provide for you."

"We're separated, Nick. Just because I haven't

filed for divorce, yet..." She stopped because she didn't want to discuss why she hadn't filed for divorce.

"And you think by taking an apartment in Kansas City, getting a job with Robbins Interiors, buying a beat-up old car that can't safely take you a block—"

"How do you know all that?" she demanded, surprised before she stopped to think. When she did use her head, the answer was appallingly clear. "You had me followed?" she asked, her eyes wide with dismay, her voice rising several octaves. How else would he know so much about her life?

"No, of course not!" When she continued to glare at him, not giving an inch, he muttered, "Just checked up on. You're my wife, Andy. It's my duty to protect you."

"I don't need your protection," she assured him. Turning, she set his dishes on the cabinet and then walked to the door. "I don't need anything from you."

"Where are you going?"

"To watch the news on television."

Bess had refused all Nick's attempts to buy her a television, but he'd finally surprised her with one for her birthday two years ago. Though she complained about it a lot, she'd finally confessed to Andrea that she "occasionally" watched a soap opera. And then proceeded to relate every plot twist for the past two years.

Andrea switched on the set and checked her watch. She had at least an hour to kill before the ten o'clock news came on. Hopefully, there'd be some program worth watching.

As she flicked through the channels, she heard a step behind her.

"Mind if I join you?"

"You? I didn't think you watched television." She didn't turn around, thinking that he might go away if she didn't look at him.

"I don't think I can make any deals tonight without a telephone or a fax, so I might as well relax."

Unable to bear being close to him, afraid he might question her more, she swung around and tossed the channel changer to him. "Here. I think I'll go to bed."

He caught her arm as she rushed past him. "Come on, Andy. Sit down and watch television. I promise I'll be quiet."

And would he also promise not to touch her? Even as briefly as he held her arm, she could feel her blood racing, heating up. He had no interest in her, but she responded to his presence like a hound after a fox.

"I really don't—"

"Andy."

That one word, softly spoken, halted her protests. With a shrug, she tugged her arm away and walked back toward the television. But she didn't sit on the sofa where she'd taken her earlier nap. No, she sat in the big chair, which was Bess's favorite spot.

Nick settled on the sofa, his long legs stretched out across the coffee table. Reading the program guide, he gave her the choices for the next hour. One of the popular hospital shows was just starting, and Andy chose it.

The problems of a modern hospital were absorbing and entertaining until halfway through the show when a guest character came through the emergency door pregnant and in labor. Nick, who'd been relaxed and absorbed, shifted his position on the couch, and Andrea noted a frown on his brow.

Almost unconsciously she covered her stomach with her hands and turned back to the television. She watched the doctors reassure the woman and then confer in private about her chances of survival.

"This is crap," Nick muttered. "How about a snack?"

"A snack?" she asked, distracted by the drama in front of her.

"Yeah. You don't want to watch this stuff. It's depressing." He stood and took her hand to tug her to her feet.

"I want to see what happens," she protested.

When she didn't respond to his pull, he dropped her hand. "Fine. I'm going to the kitchen. Shall I bring you anything?"

"I'd like an apple and a glass of milk," she said, turning her attention back to the TV.

He made a disgusted sound and left the room.

Following the plotline of the story, Andrea breathed a sigh of relief when the doctors were able to deliver a healthy baby with a promise of the mother's recovery.

"Here. What happened?" Nick asked, returning from the kitchen.

She looked up in surprise to find Nick holding the apple and a glass of milk out to her. "She had her baby and everything's fine. A little boy. See, there he is," she said, pointing toward the television set.

Nick harumphed and sat back down on the sofa. "They shouldn't use real babies. What's wrong with those parents? Babies should be home, safe in their nurseries."

"I think they have strict laws to protect the baby. And the money can provide for college later on." She bit into her apple, enjoying the juicy crunch of it. "That's not all bad. Besides, the show wouldn't be as good if you didn't get to see the pretty baby."

"Babies are a lot of trouble."

Andrea turned to look at him as he stared at the television, her heart aching. "I think a baby would be worth any trouble he caused."

Somehow they'd never discussed babies before their marriage. She'd just assumed he'd want a family, as she did. When her parents died in a car accident, she'd become an orphan at an early age. She'd been in several foster homes until she got out of high school and was on her own.

With scholarships and some money from her parents' life insurance, she'd made it through college, but she'd been lonely. In quiet moments, she'd dreamed of having her own family someday, someone to share the happiness and shoulder the pain together.

She kept her face glued to the television, not wanting to see any more rejection on his face.

Nick said nothing else and the program drew to a close. The news commentator asked them to remain tuned to that station for the latest update of the flood hitting the midwest and an up-to-the-minute weather report.

"Reporting the weather can't be that difficult if the man can spell 'rain,'" Nick muttered.

"Maybe the forecast is going to change. If the rain stops, it shouldn't take too long for things to get back to normal."

"And what's normal?" Nick growled. "You in Kansas City and me in Chicago?"

"We were talking about the weather, Nick."

"I don't want to talk about the weather. I want—"

"Shh! The news is starting. I want to hear it." She swallowed a lump in her throat and tried to concentrate on the television, but in reality, she was listening for another protest from Nick. But he surprised her and said nothing.

"Good evening. Thank you for watching. The midwest, Missouri and Kansas in particular, are experiencing the worst flooding in its history. The Mississippi River is twelve feet above flood level and the Missouri, which feeds into the larger river, is several feet higher. For more details, let's go to our reporter in St. Louis, Jason Freed. Jason..."

Watching the ravages of the flood was heartbreaking. But it brought home to Andrea just how grateful she should be to be safe, with no loved ones threatened. She might not like being trapped with Nick for a day or two, but at least she was safe in Hubbard, Missouri.

When the focus of attention was switched to the weatherman, both she and Nick leaned forward. Unfortunately, the man didn't have good news. While there was a lull in the storm at the moment, radar showed more rain on the way, for at least the next five days.

"Five days?" Andrea gasped, forgetting for a moment that she should be grateful.

"At least," Nick added with a frown. "It wouldn't be so bad if I had a phone."

A sudden idea struck her. "What about your cellular phone? I thought you carried it with you everywhere." Her breathing quickened at the thought of their being rescued.

"I haven't been back to Chicago since I left for Africa, Andy. When I heard about the floods, I came straight here from New York."

"Oh." No wonder he looked so tired. "Were you really kidnapped, or did you just get lost?"

He gave a smile that was more a bare movement of the lips than an attempt to indicate humor. "I was kidnapped."

"Why?"

"An attempt to put pressure on the government. The group who kidnapped me wanted them to release some of their members who'd been imprisoned. They thought if they took an American businessman, the U.S.A. would force their government to act.''

"And did they?"

He shrugged his shoulders. "I don't know. I escaped and found some help to get me back to civilization."

For the first time, she noticed the skin on his wrists. It appeared darker than the rest of his skin, as if it had recently been rubbed raw.

Reaching out, she ran a finger over one wrist until his hand grabbing hers awakened her to what she was doing. "I'm sorry," she whispered.

"Don't worry about it," he ordered her tightly. "It's over."

She pulled her hand free and nodded, avoiding his gaze. "Yes, it's over." And so was their marriage, their life together. And she would bear the scars for the rest of her life.

Standing, she said, "I think I'll go to bed."

"Good idea," he agreed, also rising.

Because she'd hoped he would continue watching television a little longer, she stared at him, her eyes wide.

"You're going to bed now?"

"Yeah. You want the bathroom first?" His tone was casual, as if such forced intimacy didn't bother him.

Andrea wished she could show as much cool. But she couldn't. With a nod, she rushed from the room.

A few minutes later she emerged from the bath to find Nick stretched out on Bess's big bed, his hands folded behind his head. She fought to pull her gaze from his muscular length. "Sorry if I took too long."

"Nope. It gave me time to warm the bed for you."

She almost choked as she took in his words. "W-warm the bed for me?" Swallowing, she added, "I thought you'd want this bed. After all, Bess is your aunt. I'll take the other bedroom."

"I guess you haven't looked in there yet," he said nonchalantly as he sat up.

Foreboding ran through her. "No. Is there a problem?"

"Yeah. A leak in the roof."

"Where?"

"Right over the middle of the bed. Lucky break, though. The mattress was ruined, but the carpet didn't suffer. I dragged the mattress out to the garage and put a pot under the leak to catch the drip."

Lucky break. *Yeah, right.* She gathered her scattered wits around her and turned toward the door.

"Where are you going?"

"To find some blankets and make up a bed on the sofa."

"I don't see the need for that, Andy. After all, we're not divorced yet. We can share this bed."

He stood and walked toward her, but she knew, come hell or high water, and the latter was a real possibility, she wasn't sharing a bed with Nick.

Chapter Three

Nick followed her from the bedroom to the linen closet filled with Bess's beautiful quilts.

"Andy? There's plenty of cover on the bed. It's not going to be that cold tonight."

"Good," she said as she pulled a sheet and several quilts from different shelves. "I'll need one of your pillows, please. Would you get it for me?"

"Where do you think you're going to sleep?" he demanded, his hands on his hips when she turned around.

"On the sofa."

She shut the closet door and headed toward the living room, with Nick following right behind her. She would've run if she'd thought it would do her any good. But he'd always been faster than her.

Feeling his glare in the middle of her back as she

reached the sofa, she tried to send him away. "The pillow, Nick? Would you get it for me?"

"No!" he roared, frustration lacing his voice. "I won't get the damned pillow for you. Andy, you're being ridiculous, thinking you're going to sleep here on an uncomfortable sofa when there's an entire king-size bed in the other room."

"*Thinking* I'm going to sleep here?" she repeated, her voice rising. "How are you going to stop me, Nick? Unless you learned some kidnapping techniques from your jaunt to Africa."

Too many times in their marriage, she'd given in to his dominance, wanting to please him, to keep their marriage strong. All it had done was encourage him to take advantage of her, she'd finally decided during the past lonely month. No longer would she allow him to order her around.

Her response seemed to dumbfound him. Finally, after shifting his weight several times, he muttered, "I'm trying to take care of you, Andy. You look like a small puff of wind would blow you away. You need your rest."

She stiffened her backbone against his tenderness. "Thank you, Nick, but I'll be fine on the sofa."

Turning her back to him, she began to make a bed for herself. If she worked hard at it, she could pretend she was alone, that the man she adored more than any other wasn't watching her, trying to persuade her to share his bed.

When his hands seized her shoulders and inexorably pulled her away from the sofa, she struggled against him. "Nick, what—"

"Relax. I'm going to sleep here. You go get in bed." Stepping around her, he bent over the sofa to arrange the bedding.

Tears gathered in her eyes. How could she resist such caring? Just as she was about to agree to their sharing a bed, under certain conditions, of course, a suspicion crossed her mind. Was that his plan? Charm her and get his way? *Not this time, Nick.*

"I don't think you'll fit, Nick. The sofa isn't long enough for you," she reminded him, giving a little shove with her hip as she moved to the sofa.

Unfortunately her hip didn't connect with his. Instead, it brushed against the front of his jeans and his arms surrounded her. He buried his face in her hair and muttered, "Andy."

"No!" she protested, pulling away before her desire could overpower her. She'd learned six months ago that a woman's desire could be just as powerful as a man's.

They stood there staring at each other.

"Come on, Andy," he finally whispered.

"No, I won't. We're not husband and wife anymore and—"

"Damn it, would you stop saying that?"

The pain in his voice almost awakened her sympathy, her matching suffering. Almost. "No, I can't stop saying that because it's true. And I mustn't forget it."

"Why? What did I do that was so terrible? You

muttered a lot of mumbo-jumbo that last night. Crazy things about your freedom, your time. What do you want, Andy?''

What did she want? She couldn't tell him the truth, because she couldn't have what she wanted. She already knew that. So she only told him part of the truth.

''I want me, Nick. That's all I want.''

''Another cryptic message, I suppose,'' he replied with sarcasm. ''Is this another test, like coming after you? Because I don't like to be tested, Andy. I expect my wife to trust me. Of all the people in the world, she's the one person who must trust me.''

Andy almost laughed, but she was working too hard to hold back the tears. ''I know,'' she whispered. ''I know. Go to bed, Nick.''

He didn't move. ''Come with me, Andy. I'll even promise not to touch you.''

From his voice she could tell that promise hadn't been his original intention when he'd first invited her to his bed. The shiver that coursed through her had nothing to do with the coldness. ''No, Nick. Go to bed.''

This time he did as she asked, stalking from the room as if he were a six-year-old unfairly punished. Again, Andy covered her stomach with her hands. Perhaps one day she'd see the same reaction again, with a real six-year-old.

With a faint smile, she continued preparing her bed, trying to think about the future, not the past.

A soft thud pulled her from her thoughts and she

saw the white pillow as it landed on the other end of the sofa. She looked up to discover Nick glaring at her from the doorway.

"Thank you for remembering," she called softly.

"You're welcome," he muttered, and closed the door with extra emphasis.

Andrea settled among the covers, her head resting on the pillow, and smiled again. Yes, definitely a six-year-old. But one who was well nigh irresistible. She'd be well advised to keep her distance.

Andrea awakened the next morning with the covers twisted around her and one foot exposed, her toes feeling frozen. She sat up to cover the poor cold foot and realized she hadn't brought any crackers to bed with her.

"Rats!" she moaned, and made a run for the kitchen sink.

The next few moments were unpleasant, but she'd grown used to the morning routine. It served her right for not remembering the crackers. When she did, she was sometimes able to avoid the daily upheaval.

She was washing her face when she heard footsteps behind her. Whirling around, she discovered a frowning Nick.

"Did I wake you? I—I woke up starving and thought I'd fix some breakfast," she said brightly, hoping to fool him.

"I'm not surprised. You didn't eat enough dinner last night. Sit down and I'll fix breakfast." He moved toward her so she hurried out of his way.

"I didn't know you could cook." They'd had a housekeeper, one who'd been with Nick a number of years. Andrea didn't think he'd ever seen the inside of a kitchen.

"Of course, I can cook. Do you think Aunt Bess would forget to teach me?" He was bent over, searching, she supposed, for a frying pan. Andrea shook her head when she realized her gaze was concentrated on his well-defined butt instead of their conversation.

"Um, if you're going to cook, I think I'll go back to bed. I didn't sleep too well." Besides, if he fried bacon, she was afraid she'd have another round of sickness.

He gave her a strange look as she edged toward the door. "Are you sure you're feeling all right?"

She nodded, afraid to trust her voice.

"Okay, go back to bed. I'll bring you your breakfast when it's finished. In fact, go get in Bess's bed where you'll be more comfortable."

Her eyes widened and she struggled to find an answer.

"I'm not planning on joining you," he added. "You've made your point."

He thought she didn't want him? Before she could burst into hysterical laughter at the idea, she whirled and left the room. She hesitated, though, when she reached the foot of the big bed. The slight indentation in the center of the mattress, where Nick always slept, filled her with longing. Rounding the bed, she reached out and touched that area, not really surprised to find a lingering warmth.

Her mouth watered as she remembered the nights wrapped in Nick's arms. He was hot enough to heat all of Chicago, she reflected, and then giggled. And that could be taken several ways.

"You okay?" Nick called.

Quickly she scrambled into the bed and pulled up the covers. She didn't want him checking on her. "Yes, I'm fine," she shouted. "I'm in bed."

Now if she could only keep from throwing up when he brought her the unwanted breakfast, she'd count it a successful morning.

When she awoke the next time, she could've eaten anything Nick cooked, but there was no Nick in sight and she could smell nothing cooking. A quick check of her watch showed that she'd slept several hours.

"Nick?"

He appeared in the doorway, dressed in tight jeans and another sweatshirt. "You're awake."

"Yes. I'm sorry I fell asleep while you were cooking breakfast. You changed clothes. Where did you find those?"

"Down in the basement. I left them here a long time ago. At least it's a change from the overalls. Are you hungry now?"

"Starved." Her gaze kept traveling up and down him, drinking in his masculine appeal.

"I'll start lunch."

He turned to go and Andrea called out to him. "I'll fix lunch if you want, Nick."

"Nope, I'll do it. There isn't a lot else to do."

"Do I have time for a quick shower?"

"Sure. Take your time."

She took Nick at his word. The only thing that drove her from the eye-awakening steamy shower was the growl from her stomach. She had discovered that once she was past the morning sickness, her hunger was incredible.

When she joined Nick in the kitchen, he had the food on the table. "I'm so impressed with your domestic abilities, Nick. I had no idea you were so talented."

One black brow slid up as he gave her a cool stare. "You think I should've spent my time in the kitchen instead of amassing a fortune?"

Andrea looked away from his challenge. "It might have made you appear a little more human," she finally muttered.

He slapped a plateful of food in front of her. "But it wouldn't have paid for the penthouse."

"I prefer Bess's house to the penthouse," she asserted, raising her chin in challenge.

"And the clothes, the furs, the jewels?"

"I don't believe I ever asked for those things. You told me I had to have them for your image."

"I didn't hear you complain about wearing them," he growled, joining her at the table.

She had the grace to blush. There had been a part of her that had enjoyed the luxury, she would admit, but it was a small part. "They were nice, but not—" She broke off. Their conversation was pointless. And painful.

"Not what? Obviously they weren't important

enough to hold you, unless you have plans to buy your own with the divorce settlement.'' The bitterness in his voice was reflected on his face, turning his handsome features into something to be feared.

The sandwich he fixed for her tasted like cardboard as she thought of her response. She didn't want his money, or at least, not much of it. But she couldn't make the dramatic statement that he could keep all of it. She'd need some help.

''Hit the nail on the head, didn't I?'' he persisted. ''Somehow I hadn't pictured you as a gold digger, sweetheart.''

His last word hurt. It had the sharp edge of a knife, slicing through her heart.

But she wasn't going to reveal such weakness. ''I guess it just proves even the great Nicholas Avery can make mistakes.'' She tried to avoid looking at him, but out of the corner of her eye she saw his hard, speculative gaze concentrated on her face.

''So, how much do you want? We can get the preliminary discussions out of the way now, since we have so much time. Save on the lawyers's fees.'' He leaned back in his chair and crossed his arms over his chest, leaving the sandwich on his plate untouched.

To stall the necessity of answering him, she took another bite of her sandwich. All that vaunted hunger had disappeared, but chewing was preferable to their conversation.

When she didn't respond, he leaned forward, narrowing the distance between them. ''Come on, Andy, I bet you've got a figure in mind. Probably had from the moment you met me. Was that the plan? Get a ring on your finger and then take me for all I'm worth?''

His words stung. She'd been so in love with him when they'd married, she'd hardly been aware of his financial position. It hadn't mattered.

"If that had been the case," she finally said, "I wouldn't have left without packing up all the jewelry, furs and clothes you think I wanted."

"I figured it was too much trouble to get the furs out of storage. After all, you won't need them until next winter. Maybe you expected me to ship them to you."

Shoving her chair back from the table, she stood and glared at him. "Keep those furs for your next bedmate. I won't be needing them."

He caught her hand as she tried to leave the table. "You haven't finished your sandwich."

"You haven't begun yours. Maybe you poisoned them to rid yourself of an unwanted wife."

"You're being ridiculous."

"No more ridiculous than your accusations of greed," she wailed, hard-fought tears finally filling her eyes. For him to cheapen what they had shared early in their marriage hurt. But maybe he was right. If it could fall apart so quickly, maybe it wasn't worth much.

She slipped from his grasp and headed for the living room. Some solitude wouldn't come amiss. Strange how crowded two people could make a house, or how alone a person could be in a crowd.

She crossed to the front window to stare out at a dripping world. Soft rain was falling now, but even as she watched, it gathered in intensity, drumming down on the soaked earth and the remains of her car. Its thundering on the roof helped drown out her thoughts, too. Good. She was tired already of facing the past.

"Come back and eat, Andy. We won't talk, but you need your food. You scarcely ate last night."

She didn't turn around. "I'm fine."

When he left the room, she felt even more alone. She'd told him to go. What was wrong with her? She knew what was wrong. Even though she was the one who left, she hadn't wanted to go. Hadn't wanted to live apart from him. Hadn't wanted him to hate her.

The door opened again, and her heart leaped. She heard his footsteps behind her, but still she stubbornly watched the outside world.

"Here's your food. I added a glass of milk. You can use the calories. While you eat, I'm going outside to gather up some wood to dry out on the back porch in case the electricity goes out."

She turned around in time to see his tall shoulders pass through the door before he closed it behind him. Her gaze fell on the sandwich and she wandered over to it, a resurgence of her earlier hunger and a fit of reasonableness prompting her.

He was right. She did need the calories. And not just for herself. She cradled her stomach, not quite as flat as it had been a month ago. She was six weeks pregnant when the morning sickness began, alerting her to a change in her body. It should have been a happy time. Instead she'd been miserable with indecision and fear.

Only the week before, she and Nick had discussed a family. He'd been adamant about not wanting a baby. Then the night before she'd left, they'd had their first real argument. She couldn't believe her dream of a family was unachievable.

But he'd convinced her.

No baby. Not now, not ever. He wanted no children to carry on his name, his company. As inscrutable as ever, he'd refused to give any reasons.

The first morning Andrea had woken up ill, she'd attributed it to nerves. But the morning after their argument, when she again threw up, something had prompted her to buy a pregnancy test kit. And it was true. In spite of all the precautions Nick had taken, she was pregnant.

His feelings about a child, on top of his refusal to let her share any of his life beyond the bedroom, had destroyed any hope for the future, their future. As much as she loved Nick, she could not allow her child to be unwanted. Her life as a foster child, after her parents' death when she was ten, had made her promise herself her child would always be wanted.

Suddenly her frustrations and the heartaches of the past six months crystalized into a determination to protect the life growing in her. Within minutes, her decision had been made. She packed her things, the clothing and mementos she'd brought into the marriage, and she'd left.

And had not heard a word from Nick until he'd walked into Bess's house a month later. Except for the money he'd deposited into her account.

She wandered back to the window, sandwich in hand, to stare at the hypnotizing rainfall, which emphasized their isolation. Just her and Nick. No one else in the world. And they couldn't get along.

Good thing Adam and Eve were more compatible, she thought derisively, or the human race might have gotten off to a very slow start. Or not made it at all.

She caught a glimpse of movement out of the corner of her eye and wondered if Nick had come around the house in the rain. Studying the area just beside the porch, she saw nothing and almost turned away when again some action caught her attention.

Peering through the rain, a small brownish-yellowish blob wriggled against the bottom step. Even as Andrea watched, a small paw reached the top of the bottom step before slipping off.

With a frown, Andrea put down her sandwich and ran to the front door and opened it, the din of noise from the rain surrounding her as she did so. The wind was strong, buffeting her as she trod carefully to the steps. Rain was blowing in her face, making it difficult to see, but the pitiful animal, exhausted from its struggles, was visible. A puppy.

Without any more hesitation, Andrea was down the steps in seconds, scooping up the whimpering animal and returning to the safety of the house. Closing the door behind her, shutting out the turmoil that surrounded them, she cuddled the small animal against her.

"You poor baby. Where did you come from?" Though she didn't expect an answer, the sound of her voice reminded her of the needs of the puppy. She hurried to the linen closet and took out a towel. Wrapping the puppy in it, she rubbed and massaged it, laughing when his little head poked out and a pink tongue lathered her hand.

Food seemed the next need after warmth, and she carried her small burden to the kitchen. Opening a tin of canned milk, she poured the liquid into a small bowl, heated it briefly in the microwave and held it under the puppy's nose. In no time, the animal had licked the bowl dry.

"My goodness, you're so fast," she exclaimed, and cuddled the puppy against her cheek. "Would you like some more?"

Since his tongue was licking her cheek, she took that as a yes and prepared more milk for him, as well as small bits of bread to soak in it. Again he finished off the bowl. With his tummy full of food and wrapped in a towel, he settled down on Andrea's lap and promptly went to sleep.

Without thinking, she ran her fingers over his soft warm fur, enjoying the feel of him. "You poor little creature," she crooned, "to be lost in that huge storm. No wonder you were frightened. Don't worry, I'll protect you."

He had no collar or tags, and she wasn't sure he was old enough to be away from his mother. She'd

never had pets in the foster homes, but she'd promised herself when she was settled, she'd get a pet.
Instead her attention had been captured by Nick.

''You'll be welcome company. I've been lonely the
past month. In fact, we can snuggle together in bed.
Would you like that?''

She hadn't heard the kitchen door open behind her,
but Nick's voice wasn't soothing as he roared, ''Who
the hell are you talking to?''

Chapter Four

Nick's abrupt, angry question caused Andrea to jump, clutching the puppy tightly against her. Frightened, the puppy awakened and started clawing Andrea's arm in a frantic attempt to save itself from whatever danger had awakened it.

"There, baby, it's all right," Andrea murmured, stroking its soft fur before turning to face Nick. "I was talking to the puppy."

Though he was still frowning, Nick's features lost some of their tension. "Where did the dog come from?"

"I found it by the front porch, trying to find a dry spot. Isn't it darling?"

"You mean it's not Aunt Bess's? This is just some wild dog you picked up? How can you be so silly, Andy? You might have been bitten." He stepped forward as if he would take the dog from her.

Andrea backed away. "What do you think you're going to do? Toss it back out in the storm?"

"I'll put it in the shed. It'll stay dry there."

Andrea noticed there was no concern in his voice for the puppy. Just a practical decision. "No! Then I'd have to get wet going out to feed it. I want to keep it here in the house." She cuddled the puppy on her shoulder and it licked her cheek, as if it knew she was fighting for its life.

"You're being foolish. The dog looks too young to have even had its shots. What if it bites you?"

"It won't bite me." After giving Nick a wary look, she sat back down in her chair.

Nick stared at her, continuing to frown, but she pretended he wasn't even there.

"You need to change. You're all wet, I suppose from saving that mongrel. Did you finish your lunch?" Nick looked around the kitchen, as if searching for her dishes.

She thought guiltily of the almost-untouched sandwich in the living room. She had *intended* to eat, but the puppy had distracted her. "I'll...I'll finish it in a minute."

"Go change first," he ordered imperiously.

She was going to argue with him, just to let him know that he no longer had any control over her actions, but a sneeze made her think twice about such behavior. Without a word, she got up to leave the room.

"Leave the dog here," he ordered again as she rose to retreat to the bedroom.

"Oh, no. You'd throw him out, you heartless creature. The puppy goes with me."

Nick grumbled but said nothing until she'd almost reached the door. "Wait a minute. He's not house trained. You'd better not let him on the bed, because I'll throw him out for sure if he has an accident in the one dry bed in the house."

Having won the argument over keeping the dog put Andrea in a good mood. "I won't let him mess up your bed," she promised and hurried from the room.

Of course, she couldn't prevent the untrained puppy from doing exactly what Nick had warned, but it wasn't on the bed, and she carefully cleaned up the mess. Once she and the puppy were both dry, she went to the living room to finish her lunch.

The sandwich, along with the plate it had occupied, was gone. She'd make another one, she decided, and headed to the kitchen.

Nick was standing at the back door, staring out its window at the heavy rain falling nonstop. Her sandwich was sitting on the table, along with the glass of milk she'd started drinking. Without a word, she sat in front of her meal, the puppy in her lap, and began to eat.

When she'd finished, Nick pulled out a chair and sat beside her. "How about some cookies to finish off your meal?"

"No, thanks, I couldn't. Maybe I'll have some later for an afternoon snack." She wanted to rise and leave Nick alone, but where would she go? In the living room to watch television?

"What are you going to do with that thing?"

She followed the direction of his eyes to the puppy sleeping in her lap. With a smile she said calmly, "Keep him."

"Why?"

"I've always wanted a puppy. The foster homes I was in didn't allow pets, so I've never had one." She couldn't help beaming at him. "For the first time in my life, I get to have a puppy. What should I call him?"

His lips curled up on one side, forming a quirky smile. "How about Rat? He looks like a drowned rat right now."

"Nick!" she protested, but not too vigorously since it was clear he was teasing her. "He's going to be a beautiful dog. What kind do you think he is?"

"Definitely a mixture. I imagine he'll be fairly large, too. You'll need something bigger than your apartment if you're going to keep him."

She frowned, thinking about his words. It was a struggle to pay the rent for the apartment she had. Something larger, for the sake of her pet, was impossible. "It'll be a while before he grows too large, won't it?"

As much as she'd tried to hide them, her worries must have come through.

"Don't worry about it," Nick muttered. "I'll find you a house with a yard…if you're determined to stay in Kansas City."

"I can't—you can't—never mind. I'll manage." Before she could move, Nick leaned forward and caught her upper arms. "How? How will you manage, Andy? And what's wrong with me helping you? I'm your husband."

"It doesn't matter how I manage, Nick, but I will. And just an hour ago you were accusing me of trying to take you for all you've got. Be grateful I'm refusing!"

She pulled herself from his hold and stood.

"Where are you going?"

"To the living room."

She heard him taking her dishes to the sink as she left the kitchen and was relieved that he'd found something to do. Nick's constant supervision was the last thing she needed.

Her relief was short-lived. Curled up on the sofa, resting against the pillow she'd left from last night, with the puppy resting in her lap, she was content for all of two minutes until Nick entered the room.

"Want me to turn on the television?"

"No, thanks, unless there's something you want to see," she said politely, hoping there wasn't.

"No." He sat in Bess's big chair and stared at her.

Uneasy, Andy searched for an innocuous subject that would eliminate any talk of her finances, her future or their marriage. "I still haven't thought of a name for the puppy."

"Too bad we don't know what Noah called the dogs on the ark. That would be appropriate since we're being flooded, too."

Inspiration hit her. "Thanks, Nick. I can call my puppy Noah. Don't you think that's a great name?"

She bent to kiss the puppy's head. "How about that, Noah? Do you like your new name? And just like Noah, you survived the flood."

"With your help. I hope he realizes he owes his life to a soft touch like you." Nick still sounded irritated, but something else in his words caught Andrea's attention.

"Is he a boy, Nick? I've never had a dog so I—"

Nick surprised her by lifting the dog. He immediately replaced him in Andrea's lap. "Yeah. It's a he."

"Did you have puppies when you were a boy?" she asked curiously, wondering about his detachment.

At first she thought he wouldn't answer her. During their brief marriage he'd seldom ever talked about himself, his past.

Finally he leaned back in the chair and said, "Yeah, I had a dog. He died when I was seventeen."

"What was his name?"

"Barney."

"Didn't you get another dog after Barney died?" she whispered, fascinated with a chance to find out more about Nick.

"No."

"Why?"

"I was going off to school the next year. It didn't seem like a good idea."

"But surely Bess would've kept it while—"

"No! Bess didn't need a dog."

She wasn't hearing all the story, she knew. Even though she was sure he wouldn't want to answer her question, she asked, "Did Barney die of old age?"

"No. Let's turn on the television."

He didn't move. Neither did she. "Why did your dog die?"

Slowly he looked at her, his eyes glacier-hard. "My father ran over Barney one night when he came home drunk. When he realized what he'd done, he tossed the dog into a ditch and mentioned it over breakfast the next morning."

The callousness of his father's behavior horrified her and explained Nick's attitude. "Oh, Nick, I'm sorry!" she exclaimed.

"It was a long time ago."

"But—" She'd started to protest, but Nick's gaze stopped her. She ducked her head and stroked the puppy. "Do you want to hold Noah?"

"No. I'm not a little boy anymore, Andy. A puppy isn't what I want to stroke."

They were in dangerous territory again. She sucked her breath in sharply, unable to forget the feel of Nick's hands on her body. "Don't, Nick."

"I don't see why. Even if you're going to divorce me, we're still married now. Legally, morally, there's no reason not to enjoy ourselves." The stubborn look she'd come to recognize early on in their marriage filled his face.

"But I don't want to, Nick. That's the reason we're not going to, as you put it, enjoy ourselves. You'd be the only one having a good time." She purposefully didn't look at him, hoping he wouldn't see the lie in her gaze. She'd enjoy it. She always had. But afterwards she'd hate herself for having given in.

"Don't tell me you didn't enjoy our lovemaking, Andy. I won't believe you," he protested roughly, his voice deepening.

"Fine. I won't tell you," she snapped, angry that he knew her weaknesses so well. "I won't tell you anything. Just go away and leave me alone!"

Much to her surprise, he did just that.

Andrea spent the rest of the afternoon in the living room, playing games with Noah until he grew tired. Without warning, after chasing her around the sofa, he curled up into a little ball and closed his eyes.

At first she panicked, afraid he might be ill, but the even cadence of his breathing convinced her he was just tired, having spent all his energy playing. She'd have to remember that when the baby came along. It, too, would tire easily.

With a rueful grin, she stretched out on the sofa. Maybe she'd take another nap. Her energy was at a low now too, since she was pregnant. That sounded more profitable than seeking out Nick.

She dozed lightly for about an hour. When she awakened, her first thoughts were about Nick. The story he'd told about his dog was sad. But she realized he'd revealed something else about his family. His father drank...a lot.

Never a heavy drinker, Andrea had had a glass of wine occasionally. But she discovered Nick never consumed alcohol. She'd asked him about it once, but he'd said he was driving. Since her parents had been killed by a drunk driver, destroying her life, she'd admired him for his care. Could there be more to his decision?

She stirred, restless, and a tiny yelp recalled her attention to Noah. "Hello, sweetie. Are you awake? Me, too."

She checked her watch and realized it was almost dinnertime. Scooping up the puppy, she rose and walked to the kitchen.

Just inside the door, she stopped, surprised to find Nick playing solitaire at the kitchen table. "I didn't know Bess had cards."

He raised one eyebrow but said nothing, continuing to flip through the cards.

Determined not to let his grumpy mood influence her, she asked cheerfully, "Are you winning?"

"No."

She sighed and moved over to open the refrigerator. "You're hungry?" Nick asked.

"It's almost time for dinner. I thought I'd start a meal. Don't you want something to eat?"

"Yeah, but I'm tired of sandwiches," he muttered.

"I could make a casserole with the left-over turkey, if you'll hold Noah."

He glared at her, as if she were up to some trick. "He can sit on the floor."

"No, he'd be under my feet constantly. He's still frightened." She snuggled the puppy to her face for a kiss before looking at Nick. "Please?"

"Put him in the bedroom."

"He'd cry and I couldn't stand it."

He continued playing his card game, refusing to

look at her, but Andrea stood silently, watching him. Finally he threw the extra cards down on the table. "All right. Give me the damned dog."

"You have to promise to be nice to him," she warned sternly. But she was smart enough not to wait for an answer. After petting Noah again, she put him into Nick's large hands. The puppy whimpered as she moved toward the sink, as if unsure of his place.

"Pet him, Nick, so he won't cry, or I'll never get dinner fixed."

Much to her surprise, Nick did as she asked, settling the puppy against his chest in one hand, the other stroking him gently. "It's a good thing we didn't have kids. You would've spoiled them rotten," he rumbled.

Fortunately, he wasn't looking at her. Andrea quickly erased her stricken expression and turned her back to the man and dog.

After dinner Andrea asked, "Would you like to play cards instead of watching television tonight?"

Nick rose to help clear the table. "What kind of card games can you play?"

"Gin is about the only game for two people."

"All right. Gin it is. Are we playing for money?"

His quick acceptance of her suggestion left Andrea breathless. They'd never played games together while they were married. In fact, in the past twenty-four hours, they'd spent more time together, done more talking, than they ever had the entire six months they'd been married.

"No, not for money. How about we play for who does the cooking tomorrow?"

"That's a deal, because I'm going to win and I think you're the better cook."

"You're awfully confident, aren't you?" she asked with a grin. "I happen to be a great gin player."

He shot a look her way that she recognized. An all-conquering, superior male look that said he would win.

Determination filled her and she sat and took the deck of cards from his hands to shuffle. Noah, in her lap, as usual, struggled from his drowsy state to poke his nose toward the deck of cards as she expertly dealt them.

"Taking charge, are you?" Nick asked softly, a smile on his lips. "Even with Noah's help, you're dead meat, sweetheart."

Unperturbed, Andrea arranged her cards. "You say the nicest things, Nick," she cooed in return. "Discard."

Several hours later Andrea had to admit defeat. Nick had won but only by the narrowest margin. More satisfying than the score was the enjoyment their playing and talking had given both of them. Nick was relaxed, grinning at his win.

"All right, I lost, but I almost won," she said.

"You're right. You're a better player than I gave you credit for. Next time, I'll be more careful about what I bet."

"Aha! You thought you had a sure thing, didn't you?"

"Yeah," he replied, but his face suddenly grew serious. "Just like when I married you."

She stared into his blue eyes, mesmerized by the pain she saw there. She hadn't wanted to hurt him. Her hand splayed itself across her stomach. No, she hadn't wanted to hurt him, but he was an adult. Her baby, *their* baby, needed her protection more than Nick did.

"I think it's time for bed," she said abruptly, refusing to respond to his words. "I'm going to take Noah to the porch to see if he's learned anything today."

Gathering the puppy, she stood and rushed out the back door, anxious to escape Nick. She set the puppy down on the wooden planks and absentmindedly watched it sniff its way around the porch. Suddenly she realized it was no longer raining. Rushing to the edge of the porch, she looked up at the dark sky and for the first time in days saw several twinkling stars.

"Nick! Nick, come here!"

He slammed the door almost off its hinges as he rushed to her side. "What is it? Are you hurt?" He grabbed her shoulders.

"No! Look!"

"What?" he demanded, staring intently into the darkness.

"Nick, look at the sky. There are stars. And no rain! Do you think it's finally over?"

Tension flowed out of him and he draped one arm over her shoulders. It was such a comforting feeling she couldn't help sagging against him.

"I don't know. But I think I'd better see if I can fix the roof, just in case." He turned loose of her and stepped down the stairs.

Startled, Andrea protested. "Now? It's dark, Nick. You can't fix the roof in the dark."

"Bess has a good flashlight. Get it for me, will you? It's on the top shelf of the pantry." He didn't wait for her agreement, moving across the yard to a shed.

"But—" she began and then realized he wasn't listening to her. She decided getting the flashlight would be the first thing to do. Then she would argue with Nick again.

It took only seconds to find the flashlight and return to the porch. But in that space of time, Noah had managed to find the steps and was halfway down the four eight-inch challenges to his little body.

"Noah! Stop that at once!" she ordered sternly and was inordinately pleased when he paused in his explorations, as if he recognized his name.

"Did you get the light?" Nick called from inside the shed.

"Yes, just a minute." She stooped to scoop up her puppy and step into the soggy mess that was now Bess's backyard.

She stepped through the open door of the shed and shined the beam of light around the small building. Nick muttered a thanks and reached for the ladder leaning against the wall.

"Nick, I don't think you should try to repair the roof at night. You could hurt yourself."

"Don't be silly, Andy. I'm not going to do anything complicated. If it continues to rain, that leak will do a lot more damage than what it did to the mattress."

"But, Nick, if we listened to the weather report, we might find out that the rain is stopping. Then it wouldn't hurt to wait until tomorrow."

"Sweetheart, when you saw those stars, did you notice they were in the east? Did you see any in the west, where the storms come from?"

"No," she said slowly, thinking about the implications of his words. "But Bess's porch faces the east. I couldn't see to the west."

"Well, I looked before I came in here. The west is pitch dark with occasional lightning. So what do you think? Is the storm over?"

"No," she mumbled, depression settling over her.

"Lead the way out," he ordered, shifting the ladder to his right shoulder. Then he bent to pick up a hammer and a small stack of composition shingles.

"Shall I carry anything?"

"No, just the light. After all, you have Noah to manage. Why did you bring him out here?"

"Because while I was getting the light, he was preparing to explore the western world as we know it." She was rewarded by a laugh from Nick, even if it was a slight one.

Once they were out of the shed, Nick headed for the area of the roof over Bess's second bedroom. Though Bess's house was small, the roof had a fairly steep pitch, providing for high ceilings to keep the rooms cool. It looked incredibly dangerous to Andrea. Particularly in the dark.

Nick placed the ladder against the edge of the house and turned to Andrea. "I'm going to need to take the flashlight up with me. You can go back in the house where you'll be safe."

She stared at him. "You're out of your head if you think I'm going to go sit down in front of the television while you risk your life out here!"

"I'm not risking my life, Andy. I'm just climbing up to fix a leak. It's no big deal. Besides, you wanted to watch the weather." While he talked in that maddeningly calm voice, he stuck the hammer in a loop on the old overalls he'd changed back into, put nails in a front pocket and tucked the loose shingles under one arm. "These old overalls are coming in handy," he added, grinning at her.

She almost wept. The old Nick, the one who had won her heart, was smiling at her. She wanted to throw her arms around him and beg him never to leave her. But she couldn't, because he already had. The longer they were married, the less she'd seen that grin. Nick had seemed to grow more and more solemn, tense, with each passing day.

Taking a step back, she thrust the flashlight at him. "Here."

He took the light but stared at her curiously. "Are you all right?"

"I'm fine. Just…just be careful."

Chapter Five

"I always am," Nick assured her. "Move away from the ladder."

She automatically obeyed him and then thought about his words. He wanted her to move so she wouldn't be hurt if the ladder fell. "I'll hold the ladder for you."

"Not necessary. It looks sturdy enough to me." Without turning around, he began climbing the old wooden ladder.

Not saying anything to Nick, Andrea put Noah back on the porch. "Stay there," she whispered, shaking her finger at the puppy. Then she moved back to the ladder and grabbed hold of it.

When Nick reached the roof and had to leave the confines of the ladder, Andrea felt a ridiculous loss, as if they had parted once again, but she told herself she was being silly. With her heart in her mouth, she watched him inch his way up the roof. When he'd reach about halfway between the ladder and the top of the house, he sat and began pulling out the material from his overalls.

One nail got away and rolled down the roof, picking up pace. Andrea ducked as it flew past her head, but Nick, craning to see what had happened, discovered her at the ladder.

"Andy! Get away! I thought you were on the porch!"

"I'm holding the ladder."

"Damn it, Andy! That could've been my hammer. Move away!"

He had a point. She moved farther out into the yard so she could see him more clearly. "Okay. I'm safe here."

"That's not what— Fine! But stay put. Don't come any closer."

"I won't," she promised, adding to herself, *until you start down the ladder again.*

Nick's efficiency surprised her, but then she wondered why. She'd never seen him fail at anything. Except marriage, she reminded herself.

Much to her relief, the repairs only took a few minutes. Already sprinkles of rain were starting. When Nick again pocketed his supplies and started moving back down the roof, she breathed a sigh of relief.

Then he slid.

With a scream, she ran back to the ladder, hoping

to help him in some way. However, he pulled himself to a stop just a couple of feet from the edge.

"Nick! Are you okay?"

"I'm fine. Andy, I told you to move back!"

"Don't be ridiculous. Can you reach the ladder? Should I move it?"

"No, I can reach it. Get on the porch."

She ignored him, as before, grasping the ladder with both hands. The creaking and groaning of the wood as his weight settled on it made Andrea uneasy, but the ordeal was almost over. She didn't understand how wives of policemen and firemen were able to stand the fear their husbands' jobs brought.

Nick quickly moved down the ladder and Andrea was about to step away from it to let him reach the ground when the fourth rung from the bottom gave way. Nick fell straight to the ground with a groan before collapsing on Andrea, knocking them both into the mud, and the ladder landed on top of them.

Stunned, Andrea's first conscious thought occurred when Noah licked her face. "Noah! What are you doing off the porch?" she scolded weakly. Then what had happened hit home. "Nick? Nick, are you all right?" she cried, wrapping her arms around him.

"Andy, damn it, I told you to stay back. Did I hurt you?" Though his words were the old Nick, his voice was faint, almost blurred.

"I'm fine." She suddenly remembered the baby, but she felt all right. There was no pain. With a sigh of relief, she shifted slightly from underneath Nick, because Nick had braced himself with his arms, his weight hadn't really fallen on her. "Are you sure you're not hurt?"

"I don't know. My ankle hurts."

"Can you move to your right so I can get up?"

With a grunt, he managed to follow her suggestion and she slipped from beneath his heavy weight. When she stood, she shoved the ladder to the side, then picked up Noah and set him back on the nearby porch. "Stay!" she commanded in her sternest voice.

Then she turned back to Nick, who was trying to sit up. "Did you hit your head, Nick?"

"I don't think so. At least, if I hit it, it was on you."

"Can you get up?" she asked, taking his arm. "It's beginning to rain again."

"Rain might be preferable to the mud I'm wallowing in." In spite of his words, he struggled to stand. When he put weight on his left ankle, however, he cringed in pain and tried to balance on his right foot.

"Is it broken?" she asked, frightened that she might have to set a broken bone. Her medical knowledge was nil.

"I don't think so. Probably just sprained. But getting me into the house is going to be hell. You're too little."

"No, I'm not." She crossed over to his left side and slid an arm around his waist. "Come on. It's only a couple of feet to the porch."

Once they reached the porch and made it up the steps, the rest of the trip into the house was easy. Nick hopped on his good leg all the way to the bathroom.

Andrea only paused to pick up Noah before following him.

She reached past him to turn on the hot water. "Can you undress alone?"

"Yeah." He began unfastening the straps to the overalls and Andrea moved to the door.

"I'll see if I can find you more underwear and a T-shirt to sleep in."

She was a soggy mess and couldn't wait for her own shower, but she had no intention of joining Nick. The injured should go first. She hurried to the basement to look for more spare clothes.

Noah complained about being tucked under her arm, but she certainly wasn't going to put him down. He was as muddy as her and Nick. There was going to be enough to mop up once she got the three of them cleaned. She didn't want more.

She thrust the clean clothes through the bathroom door while the shower was still running. "Here are your clothes!" she shouted. The T-shirt had actually been a nightshirt of Bess's, pink with a big red heart on it, but it was roomy and clean. Beggars couldn't be choosers.

Waiting by the door, Andrea wasn't surprised to hear Nick's complaint when he emerged.

"I'm supposed to wear this?" He gestured to the nightshirt that enveloped him.

Andrea was glad to see it came halfway down his strong thighs. She didn't need any more of his body exposed than necessary. "At least it's clean and roomy. And no one will see you but me." She sent him a grin that promised some teasing. Then she sobered. "How's your ankle?"

"It will be better when I'm in bed," he assured her, his voice showing his exhaustion.

"I've turned down the covers. Come on." She led the way toward the bed.

"I'll manage. You get in the shower. You're soaked and muddy."

Since he was demonstrating his ability to get to the bed on his own, Andrea followed his orders. She wasn't feeling all too well herself.

Under the stream of warm water, she perked up. Noah, however, didn't like the spray of the shower. As soon as all the mud was off his sleek fur, she set him down on the bathroom floor. "Don't get into trouble," she warned him.

When she emerged from the shower, she felt much better, though she was exhausted. After dressing quickly, she and the dog gave Nick a visit.

"I think we need to elevate your leg," she decided, frowning at the swollen ankle.

"Probably," he mumbled, more than half asleep.

She fetched two quilts from the closet and built a mound for his ankle. Then she took several small towels to the bathroom and wet them down. Somewhere in the back of her mind cold compresses seemed important.

"Hey!" Nick shouted, coming awake when the cold, wet towels hit his ankle.

"Shh! I'm doctoring you," she protested. "Here,

hold Noah.'' She thrust the dog into Nick's arms and arranged the towels to her satisfaction.

''But my foot is going to freeze.''

''I'll put another quilt over just your foot. Maybe it won't get too wet.'' As she turned to go back to the linen closet, Nick stopped her.

''I think you'd better sleep in here tonight…in case I need you.''

She was in such a state that she almost agreed without thinking. But one look at Nick's sharp blue eyes and she knew better. ''I don't think that will be necessary.''

He raised his eyebrows and grimaced, but he didn't make any protest. Andrea escaped from the room. She needed to finish taking care of Nick so she could get to bed. She wasn't feeling too well.

A good night's sleep made all the difference to Andrea. When she awoke the next morning, she quickly munched on the crackers she'd remembered to bring to the living room with her. Noah, having slept on a towel beside her, put his paws on her stomach and wagged his tail. With a grin, she fed him several small bits of cracker.

''We're going to have to talk about your begging,'' she promised, but Noah didn't seem too concerned. After the crackers were consumed, she got up and was relieved that everything stayed down. Last night's adventure seemed to have produced no ill effects, though she did still feel a little tired.

There was no sign of Nick in the kitchen, and she

tiptoed to the door of the bedroom. A slight snore told her he was still sleeping. She decided breakfast could wait until Nick awoke.

The morning news program she watched showed the horrible ravages the rain and flooding had caused. As Nick had said, they could be in worse straits. She was watching some small children being rescued by boat from the roof of their house when she heard Nick hobble into the bathroom. She waited anxiously for him to come out so she could find out how he'd fared.

"Still raining?" he rumbled when he came into the living room.

"I'm afraid so. How are you feeling?"

"I'm okay. How about you?"

"A little tired. Is your ankle still swollen?"

He was wearing socks again, so Andrea couldn't tell by looking.

"Yeah. But not as much. I think if I stay off it a day or two, I'll be all right."

She stood up from the couch. "Come lie here and watch television. I can bring your food in here."

"I'm not an invalid, Andy. I can move around."

"Better not. At least stay down today. If you're a lot better tomorrow, then you can get up and down." He grumbled but followed her suggestion.

"Now, you take care of Noah and I'll go make breakfast. I waited for you to wake up." And because her stomach had to settle, but he didn't need to know that.

"You sure you're okay?" he asked her again.

"Maybe a bruise here or there, but that's all."

As she busied herself around the kitchen, Andrea thought about Nick. He worked so hard at taking care of her, but he didn't want to share himself with her. What little she'd learned since they'd been marooned here she'd had to pry out of him. In Chicago, he'd avoided any heart-to-heart talks.

Yet he'd offered her anything she wanted that money could buy. As if it could make up for not giving of himself.

"Need any help?" Nick called, pulling her attention back to the eggs she was cooking.

"No. It's almost ready." She buttered toast and poured orange juice into the glasses. Dividing the scrambled eggs onto two plates, she then lifted the tray and backed her way through the kitchen door.

"Sorry I took so long."

"Hey, I wasn't complaining. I just worry about you when I can't see you."

"You must've stayed in a perpetual state of worry in Chicago, then," she couldn't help muttering.

He gave her a cool look over his cup of coffee. "You were safe in the apartment."

Exasperation filled her. Did he expect her to sit on a shelf until he returned, like a favorite model airplane?

"Where's the bacon?" he suddenly asked.

After a quick glance at his frown, she concentrated on her coffee.

"Sorry, but I didn't feel like cooking it this morning. It's a pain to prepare." *And the smell of it made her nauseous because of the baby.*

"I'll go cook some."

"You most definitely will not," she protested, sitting up straight and glaring at him. "I'm supposed to do the cooking today, because you won at cards. And you have to stay off your ankle."

He relaxed back against the pillow, frowning at her. "I didn't mean to upset you."

"I'm not upset. Let's watch television."

Since the only things on were soap operas and game shows, Andrea soon lost interest, but she didn't suggest another activity. Finally, she put her head down on the back of the big stuffed chair and closed her eyes.

"Andy?"

"Hmm?" she answered groggily.

"Are you sure you're all right? You've been sleeping a long time."

She discovered Nick staring at her in concern. "I have? What time is it?"

"Almost noon. Did I hurt you last night and you're not telling me?"

"No, of course not. It's just…sometimes I take naps. Besides, the television wasn't too inspiring."

"I don't know. You missed a rerun of 'Matlock.'" He grinned at her, but she noticed he still watched her.

She grimaced as she stretched, trying to get the kinks out of her body. "Darn. Let's see, 'Matlock' or a nap? That's a tough choice."

"Okay, okay," he agreed, "maybe you made the right choice, but Noah wasn't too happy about it."

Her attention immediately left Nick to focus on the puppy chewing on an edge of the sofa. "Noah! Stop that at once." He did, for all of ten seconds, and then resumed his fun. With a sigh, she picked him up. "I guess you're hungry. I'll go see what I can find for lunch."

"Want me to keep Noah in here?" he asked, surprising Andrea.

"Thanks, but I think he and I will take a trip to the back porch. I spread out some papers there. I figured we'd better start the potty training at once."

"Good idea."

While she took care of Noah's needs and then prepared lunch, Andrea realized Nick's injury was going to provide her with some privacy since he was stuck on the sofa. As long as she could manufacture things to do outside the living room, she could escape his careful eye.

Several hours later she ran out of actual work. Besides, Nick kept calling her to his side. Not that he really needed anything. She could tell he was growing more and more desperate with his reasons. The last time he said he'd lost the remote and wanted the station changed on the television.

When she discovered the remote halfway across the room on the floor, she'd known he'd thrown it there. How else would it have traveled so far? Unless he got up and placed it there. And if he could do that, he could change the channel on the television.

Finally she returned to the living room and settled back into the big chair. More soap operas filled the afternoon schedule. Or talk shows with ridiculous topics.

"Stay tuned. On 'Alex's Corner' we'll be discussing boys whose faces break out after sex. Is it in their minds or their bodies?"

"Good grief!" she exclaimed. "How can you stand such junk?"

"I don't know," Nick agreed with a smile. "Maybe we should turn the television off and read a book. Improve our minds."

With a sigh, she stood. "Good idea. Tell me what kind of book you want, and I'll look for a good one."

"How about a murder mystery? I'm in the mood to see someone get what's coming to him."

She frowned. "I'm glad you made that masculine, or I'd be worried."

She began searching the shelves across the room for a book to keep Nick interested. As she pulled several from the shelf, a third one fell to the floor.

Bending to pick it up, her gaze fell on the bottom shelf. It was filled with photo albums. She'd hadn't even realized Bess had photo albums. Certainly she'd never shown any pictures of their family to Andrea when she'd visited.

She took the books over to Nick and he approved of both of them.

"Are you going to read one of them?" he asked, selecting one to begin with.

"No. Something else caught my eye." She returned to the bookshelf and took the three volumes of photo albums. Glancing over her shoulder at Nick already involved in a book, she considered taking them to the kitchen. Somehow, she didn't think Nick would like her looking at his family history. But then again, he'd definitely notice if she left. As long as she kept quiet, he might never realize what she was looking at.

She returned to the big chair with the thick albums. Noah jumped up, clawing the material of the chair and she took him in her lap. "You're going to ruin Bess's furniture if you're not careful," she warned.

"Find something to read?" Nick asked, but his gaze never left the book he was reading.

"Yes, thanks. Let me know if I can get you anything."

"Mmm-hmm," he muttered, turning a page.

So far so good. She set two of the albums on the floor beside her chair, out of Nick's view. Then she opened the other one, eager to find out why Nick never talked about his childhood.

The first pictures were very old. Brown-and-white images taken in a studio. She studied the features of the couple in the first one. It wasn't Bess, but the lady resembled her. Could this be Nick's mother? And the dark-haired man so much like Nick must be his father.

They were a handsome couple, smiling at each other, as if they were deeply in love. Nick looked like his father. It didn't take much imagination to believe that one day Nick would look at her with such love.

Except that she'd left him, of course.

She risked a glance at him, but he was still absorbed by the murder mystery.

There was another picture, loose inside the front cover. Another photo of a couple. Andrea recognized Bess's warm smile at once. Even with wrinkles and gray hair, Bess had a smile that could fill anyone's heart. The man beside her wasn't much taller, and his cheeks were full, indicating he didn't miss many meals. There was a gentle humor in his eyes that made Andrea believe she would've liked him. This must be Homer, Bess's husband. He'd died about five years ago, but Bess talked about him a lot.

Andrea turned back to the first picture. There was love in that picture, but Nick's father didn't look…comfortable. That was the word she was searching for.

Had he been a loving father? Nick's story about his dog didn't indicate it. But surely when Nick was smaller?

"What the hell are you doing?" Nick suddenly roared.

Chapter Six

After almost dropping the photo album, Andrea heaved a sigh of exasperation. "Nick, you have to stop yelling at me. It's not good for my nervous system."

He ignored her lighthearted response. "Where did you get that?"

"The photo album? From the bookshelf."

"You have no right to look through that. It's personal." He reached over to take it from her, and she pulled back.

"You may be right about it being personal, but if it is, it's Bess's personal photo album. Are you saying she wouldn't let me look at it?" Andrea didn't need Nick's answer. Bess had given her the run of the house from her first visit.

"It's my family."

"Until our divorce, it's my family, too," she reminded him softly. "A family I know nothing about." She waited, but he made no response. "Why? Why do you never talk about your family, Nick?"

"Like most people, I avoid unpleasant subjects," he responded coolly, turning away.

"I know your mother died in childbirth. What about your father?"

Nick had buried his nose back in the murder mystery and didn't answer.

"Nick? Is your father alive?"

"No."

"When did he die?"

"Do you mind? I'm trying to read."

He obviously wasn't going to answer any questions about his family. Andrea, however, didn't let his reaction stop her. She went through the album slowly, building a history of the Avery family in her head.

The pictures of Nick growing up were particularly interesting. There were lots of photos of Bess and Nick together, usually with Bess's arms wrapped around the little boy. Sometimes Homer was with them. Only one or two pictures showed Nick with his father, and they were never touching.

"You didn't get along with your father?" she asked, watching him to see his reaction.

"No."

"Why?"

"Find a book to read, Andy. Anything would be more interesting than my childhood."

Would he say the same thing if he knew she was carrying his child? Even if he had no interest in the baby, she would want to know medical history, if nothing else. Had his father died of some disease?

With a sigh, she closed the photo album. She could ask Bess when she saw her again. Whenever that was. Standing, she walked over to the window and stared out at the pounding rain. It seemed never-ending.

A sudden bolt of lightning, accompanied by tumultuous thunder, struck a tree near the front of the house. With a scream, Andrea shielded her eyes from the light. Before she could recover from the surprise, she felt Nick's arms go around her.

"Are you all right?" he demanded, pressing her against him.

The feel of his strong body sheltering hers, consoling, loving, sent Andrea's heart into overdrive, even more than the lightning. She allowed herself the luxury of relaxing against him, hearing his heart thumping beneath her ear, feeling his taut muscles beneath her fingertips.

"I'm all right," she promised, finally raising her head to look into his blue eyes.

His gaze met hers and she couldn't turn away. Not even when she realized he was going to kiss her. His mouth lowered to hers, his lips tender, sweet, and she reached out to meet him. She didn't remember all the warnings she'd given herself, the fears. All she remembered was the longings, the long nights, the loneliness.

Quickly the nature of Nick's kiss changed to one of hunger and passion. He pulled her even closer, burying her in his warmth, urging her mouth to open to his.

Only when his hands began roaming her body, heating it to greater levels of desire, did Andrea realize she had to stop...or never stop.

She wrenched her lips from his and pressed her cheek against his chest, her face turned away. "Nick, we can't do this."

"Why not?" he asked huskily, his lips trailing down her neck.

"Because you don't want me."

There was a stunned stillness in him, telling Andrea he'd heard her words, but couldn't believe them. Then he pressed her against him, tighter. "That's a stupid remark, Andy. You can feel how much I want you."

"No," she whispered softly. "You want my body, Nick, but you don't want me. And I can't separate the two." Raising her head, she stared at him, daring him to contradict her words.

"You're talking nonsense. More of the mumbo-jumbo you came out with that last night. I want *you*, Andrea Avery, and no one else. I haven't had another woman since the day I met you. *You* are the one I want." He grasped her shoulders and shook her slightly for emphasis.

"It's not mumbo-jumbo, Nick. You don't want to talk to me, to share my life. You just want me in your bed. By the time I left, I wasn't sure you'd seen me in street clothes in a month. You only came home to sleep with me."

"I came home to make love to you. Because I love

you, Andy. But I'm a busy man. There are a lot of demands on my time. What did you think? That I let other people run my business? That I'd take time off in the middle of the day for a picnic so you could tell me about the latest soap operas you'd watched?''

The scorn in his voice hurt, but Andrea was beginning to recognize a pattern. If she got too close, demanded too much, Nick attacked. She also noticed he took a step away from her, in spite of his professed desire.

''No,'' she responded calmly, ''because I don't watch soap operas. I thought we'd talk about our future, our plans, our days.''

''Our future is what I'm working on. I don't need to discuss my business with you. What did you expect for the future? I offered you whatever you wanted!''

''No, you didn't.''

He took another step back. ''What do you mean? What did you want that I haven't offered you?''

''Yourself. And a child.''

He turned and limped from the room, slamming the door behind him.

Nick remained in Bess's bedroom the rest of the afternoon. Andrea didn't disturb him, but she did a lot of thinking. When she'd first left Nick, the pain had been so intense, thinking was beyond her. But looking back at their married life, she realized Nick's lovemaking had been as fierce as ever at the end, but the time he gave her had shrunk.

He'd still wanted her, but he'd been withdrawing.

Was it business? Had he been pressed for time? She didn't think so. What little she knew about his operations had been from his staff. She'd heard Nick's chef questioning his chauffeur about the extra hours Nick was working.

The chauffeur couldn't explain it. He'd reported that Nick frequently stayed after everyone had left the office. Sometimes just staring into space.

As if he didn't want to come home.

At the time that conversation had been another nail in the coffin of her marriage. Now she wondered if it wasn't another example of Nick's defense, just as his withdrawal today had been.

When it got late, she put aside her worries and prepared meat loaf for dinner, with canned vegetables and biscuits. After setting the table, pouring drinks and putting the food in place, she knocked on the bedroom door. "Nick? Dinner's ready."

But there was no response.

"Nick?"

"Yeah?"

"Dinner's ready."

"I'm not hungry."

With a smile on her lips, she shook her head. Men! Or one man in particular. She didn't knock again. Instead she opened the door. "Don't be ridiculous," she said calmly to the big man sprawled on the bed.

He raised up and glared at her, as if he couldn't believe she'd dared to open the door.

"Come on, Nick. We're stuck here together for who knows how long. Pouting is unacceptable."

"Just because I'm not hungry, you think I'm pouting?" he asked, outraged.

She smiled again. "No. I think you're pouting because you didn't like what I said, you've hidden in the bedroom all afternoon, and you say you're not hungry when I know you are."

Slowly the anger drained from his blue eyes and he sat up, swinging his feet to the floor. "Damn it, Andy, you make it hard to stay mad."

"Good, because I've fixed meat loaf."

"Why didn't you say so in the first place?" he demanded, rising. "That's my favorite."

"I know," she told him, smiling again.

He shook his head as he came toward her. "That's dirty pool, lady. You shouldn't tempt me like that."

"All's fair in love and war, Nick."

"Yeah. I just wish I knew which one we're having," he muttered, stopping in front of her.

"How's your ankle?"

"A little stiff, but the swelling's all gone."

"Good. You can do the dishes tonight." She turned and walked to the kitchen, with him right behind her.

"Wait a minute. That wasn't part of our deal, me cleaning the dishes."

"Nope. But if I cook, I shouldn't have to clean, too, should I? And since you're the only one here besides me, who else will clean?"

In truth, they both cleaned the kitchen after dinner. But Andrea made sure Nick did the washing of the utensils.

"How am I going to explain dishpan hands when

I get back to Chicago?'' he demanded as he washed the last of the pots and pans.

"Don't worry. It will give you the human touch. Some of those sycophants around you don't know that you are.''

He gave her a wicked grin. "I like it that way.''

"I'm not sure it's good for your soul. You need someone to keep you humble,'' she teased, drying the meat loaf pan.

After a relaxed meal and the teasing they'd indulged in, Andrea was disappointed to see Nick's expression turn serious. He looked away and then back at her again.

"That's what I had you for, Andy. Every time I thought about you, I knew I was an ordinary man with incredible luck. I was in awe of what we had.''

"In awe...or in fear, Nick?''

"You think I'm afraid of you?''

"No. I think you're afraid of...of loving me. Or anyone else, besides Bess. And I think the only reason you love Bess is that she didn't give you any choice when you were too young to know better.''

His jaw clenched. "When did you become a psychologist?''

"I haven't. But I'd be glad to talk to a psychologist to save our marriage. Would you?'' She felt like someone pressing on a bruise to prove that it was there. She knew what his response would be.

"I don't need a psychologist. If you'll remember, you're the one who left our marriage. Not me.''

She fought to suppress her anger. "When you figure out why, Nick, and want to do something about it, let me know.'' She hung the dish towel over the back of one of the kitchen chairs and turned to the back door.

''Where are you going?'' Nick demanded.

''To get Noah.''

''I forgot about him. Where is he?''

''I fixed a pen on the back porch. I don't think it's too good to let him get used to my company all the time. When I go back to work, he'll have to be alone during the day.''

Without waiting for him to respond, Andrea stepped out onto the back porch. With a frown, she realized the temperature had dropped. Instead of being cool, the night air was chilly, making her wish she had a jacket.

''Are you cold, Noah?'' she asked, kneeling beside the box she'd fixed for her new pet.

The puppy stood on its hind legs, begging with energetic squeaks for her to pick him up.

''Did you eat your dinner?'' she asked. Crumbled bits of meat loaf and bread in warm milk had held his attention when she'd left him. She checked the bowl and discovered it had been licked clean.

''Aha. Meat loaf must be your favorite, too.''

She sensed more than saw the impatient movement at the door, but Nick remained silent. She lifted Noah and gave him a kiss on his wet little nose before snuggling him against her cheek.

''Ooh!'' she exclaimed, catching her first whiff of the puppy. ''I think maybe you need a bath before bedtime. A hot shower will warm both of us up." She shivered as she turned toward the door. "Did you notice, Nick? It's colder."

"Yeah. I think I'll watch the weather."

"I'll be in after Noah and I have a shower."

He held the door open and as she walked past him, she thought he muttered, "The damn dog is being treated better than me."

By the time she and Noah reached the living room, the weatherman was in the middle of his presentation.

"What's he said?"

"Shh!" Nick cautioned, his gaze never leaving the television.

She sank into the big chair, and Noah curled up on her stomach, ready to sleep, unconcerned with man's worries. As the television flashed colorful maps, Andrea realized the forecast wasn't good. A cold front that would only increase the moisture in the air was moving in.

"How cold?" she asked.

"Below freezing," Nick muttered.

They watched the rest of the program in silence. Andrea watched Nick's face, wondering at the concern reflected there. When he got up to turn off the television set, she asked, "We'll be all right, won't we?"

"As long as the electricity works."

She'd forgotten the possibility of being without electricity. It wasn't a comforting thought. "Would you like another quilt for your bed?"

"I have those you used to prop up my foot. I'll bring you some extra covers, though. Are you sure you want to stay out here?"

"Out here?" she asked, a little confused.

"Here on the couch instead of in the bed."

"I'm sure," she said at once, a shiver going down her spine that had nothing to do with cold.

He left the room without trying to change her mind. When he brought in two more blankets, he said a quiet good-night and left.

Andrea stared after him, longing for what she couldn't have, Nick's love and the family she yearned for. That thought reminded her to collect several crackers for the morning.

"Stay here, Noah. I'll be right back," she assured the puppy as she put it on the floor.

Within five minutes the two of them were tucked in for the night, Noah's little floppy ears just sticking out from under the covers. They both fell asleep to the sound of rain beating down on the windowpanes.

Sometime before dawn, the sound changed, rousing Andrea slightly from her sleep. Sleet pounded the glass with a staccato sound, as if they were under attack from a neighboring country. She rubbed her eyes and, after she identified that the sound was harmless, drifted off again in her cozy cocoon.

The next time she awakened, Nick was building a fire in the fireplace across from the sofa.

She started to sit up and question him, but a warning heave from her stomach warned her to eat her crackers. At the first bite, Nick spun around on his heels.

"What are you doing?" he asked, puzzled.

"Um, eating a cracker. I brought them to bed with me last night because I was hungry, but then I forgot to eat them." She shoved the rest of the cracker into her mouth and chewed rapidly.

"Don't eat those now. I'll fix breakfast as soon as I've finished here."

She continued to eat her crackers, but she managed to ask a question. "Why are you building a fire?"

"Because the electricity went out and it's cold, as you'll notice as soon as you get up. You could go start breakfast, if you want. It's fortunate Bess's stove is gas instead of electric."

"Yeah," Andrea muttered, not moving except to eat another cracker. She couldn't believe Nick had bought her cracker story, but then, he'd never been around a pregnant woman before.

"By the way, Andy, I want bacon this morning, cholesterol or no cholesterol."

Just the mention of bacon had her stomach acting unruly and she chewed more cracker. "If you want bacon, you can cook it. In fact, I think I'll go back to sleep." She closed her eyes, hoping sheer determination would do the trick.

Instead, a warm hand covered her forehead. "Are you all right?" Nick asked. "You look a little flushed."

"I'm fine. I just don't want to get up yet. It's…it's too early." She only hoped she was right.

"How about I make breakfast, including a cup of hot tea for you. Then will you get up? It's already after nine."

"If you insist," she said with a calculated sigh. She thought if she had a few minutes alone, she'd be able to control her morning sickness. "Will you heat up some canned milk for Noah?"

He gave her a hard look but then agreed. "I'll even put him in his box for you."

"No! It's too cold."

"I'll put it in a corner in the kitchen, then. You were right. It's not going to be good for him to get used to you holding him all the time."

"All right," she agreed, surrendering Noah to Nick's waiting hands. The shift she made in doing so almost unleashed her nausea, and she covered her mouth with her hand.

"You okay?" he asked again, giving her a curious look.

"Yes, I'm fine. I'll be in the kitchen in a little while." *Go. Please go, before I embarrass myself.*

He took the dog and left her alone at last, and Andrea relaxed against the pillow with a sigh of relief. She had one cracker left and began crunching it, breathing deeply.

By the time the smell of bacon reached the living room, she was okay. Carefully, she sat up and noticed the cold at once as the covers slid down. "Brrr!" she shivered, then dashed for the fireplace. After warming herself several minutes, she raced for the bathroom.

With no heater, her stay was brief. She dressed,

putting on the light jacket she'd worn the first day she'd driven to Bess's. It seemed like it was years ago. She wished she'd brought warmer clothes, but the weather had been springlike before the floods started.

When she reached the kitchen, Nick was putting a plate of bacon and scrambled eggs on the table.

"There you are. I was about to come drag you out of bed."

"It's not like we have anything to rush to, Nick. I could've stayed in bed a little longer."

"I guess that's true."

"Are we going to be all right without electricity?" she asked as she sat. Noah, hearing her voice, began to cry and she started to get back up.

"Nope. The dog stays in the box during meals. You'd start feeding him from the table, and that's a hard habit to break."

"He's still a puppy, Nick."

"That's when you start training him."

"Ah, Mr. Expert. One dog and you know everything."

He said nothing, sitting across from her with a frozen look on his face, and she regretted her remark.

"You didn't answer my question. Will we be all right?" she asked again, hoping to distract him.

"Yeah. We're fortunate. Those modern houses with everything electric will have a lot of problems."

He passed the plate of eggs and bacon to her and, under his watchful eye, she served herself a small portion of eggs.

"You're not having any bacon?" he asked.

"No. I don't like it. But I'd like some toast." Nick had toasted bread in the oven, since the toaster was electric. Between it and the hot tea he'd fixed, she was satisfied.

"You need protein, Andy. To build you back up. You must not've been eating properly since you left Chicago."

"I'm eating fine. I just haven't had a lot of appetite lately." She took a small bite of eggs to appease him. "So the fireplace will keep us warm enough in the living room?"

"Yeah. The only problem we'll have will be at night. The bedroom doesn't have a source of heat, so we'll have to share the bed to keep warm."

Chapter Seven

"We'll do no such thing!" Andrea finally said, staring at Nick.

"We'll have to, Andy. The temperature could drop as low as twenty tonight."

"How do you know? You certainly didn't hear it on the television since there's no electricity."

"No, I heard it on Bess's battery-operated radio she keeps in case of storms. I listened to the weather report while I was cooking breakfast." He leaned back in his chair, relaxed, and watched her.

"There must be some other way." She stared at him, concentrating on the problem. Suddenly she grinned. "I know. You can make a pallet and sleep on the floor near the fireplace."

"Thanks a lot, Mother Teresa, for volunteering me for torture. I wouldn't be able to move in the morning if I spent the night on the floor. And there's no need to suffer when we have a king-size bed in the bedroom.'' He paused to challenge her with his blue eyes. "After all, you've said we're not going to make love because you don't like it. And I've certainly never forced a woman in my life. So where's the problem?''

"I just don't think it's a good idea," she said stubbornly, refusing to meet his gaze.

"Scared you might like it after all?" he questioned softly.

She raised her gaze to his triumphant face. "No. I lied earlier, as you very well know. I enjoyed our lovemaking. But it isn't enough. Even if we make love while we're stranded here, I won't stay married to you, Nick. So you're right. It doesn't matter if we sleep together, with or without making love. It won't change anything.''

Her honesty hurt him, she could tell, but it hurt her, too. It hurt to admit out loud that their marriage was over. Even though she'd left him, she admitted now that she'd hoped he would come after her and change, make everything right.

They were together now, even if he hadn't come after her, but nothing had changed. Their marriage wasn't right. It was as wrong as it had ever been.

His face grew cold, remote. "It's too bad you haven't been trained in business, Andrea." It was the first time since their marriage that he'd called her by her formal name. "Then you'd have learned the art of compromise. Most women would be thrilled with what I've offered you.''

"Perhaps." She swallowed and then tried to speak

lightly. "At least you'll have a lot of applicants for the position of wife as soon as I've vacated it."

"And will you have a long line at your door, willing to bare their souls for the chance to sleep with you?" he demanded, anger animating his features.

"Do you really think sex is the only important thing in a marriage? Is that all I ever meant to you?"

He jumped up from the table and walked to the back door. "It was real! A lot more real than all this talk you want. I was honest with you. I married you. What more do you want?"

With a sigh she rested her head in her hands. "I've already told you, I want you. Not just your body. Not just your money. I want to share our lives, our thoughts, our hearts."

"I managed to survive and prosper for thirty-two years without you. I can manage another thirty or forty alone." His back was rigid, his hands tucked in his pockets.

"Of course you can. But will you enjoy it? Will you feel complete if you don't share your life with someone? That's all I'm asking, Nick, is for you to open up, to share with me."

"You're asking too much."

She was afraid he was right. The likelihood of Nick letting her into his life was as good as that of the sun shining all day and warming up their frozen world.

With a sigh, she stood. "I'll clean since you cooked." There was no point in continuing the painful discussion. His last words had said it all.

"What?" he asked, turning around. "No more heartfelt pleas, no tears, no demands?"

"No," she replied simply, gathering up the dishes.

He stood silently while she cleared the table, watching her with an intensity that made her uncomfortable. Finally he moved toward her.

"I'll help."

"There's no need. It takes a minute to load the dishwasher."

"Andy, the dishwasher won't work. It's electric."

Realization struck her. "Oh. I'd forgotten." With sudden foreboding, she asked, "Is the water heater electric, too?"

"'Fraid so."

She sagged against the kitchen cabinet with a groan. "No more hot showers!"

"We can heat up water and pour it in the tub for a bath, though. The pioneers used to have to sit in a washtub and have someone pour water over them," Nick said, a small smile returning to his dark features.

"Yes, of course. I didn't mean to complain," she replied hurriedly, trying to dismiss the pictures of Nick scrunched down in a washtub, his torso bare.

"I'll put on water to heat so we can wash the dishes."

"Thanks." Another of Noah's yelps reminded her of her new pet and also gave her something to do while they waited for the water to boil. She crossed to the cardboard box that served as his pen.

"Sorry, baby, I almost forgot you. Did you eat your breakfast?"

As with last night, his bowl had been licked clean.

"We may have to change your name to Goliath if you keep eating so much," she warned him.

"I see you're keeping the biblical theme," Nick commented. "That will please Bess. Maybe you could even con her into adopting Noah."

"No!" Andrea answered sharply, cuddling Noah against her. "He's mine. We'll manage in the apartment until I get something bigger."

Nick opened his mouth, probably to once again offer to pay for her housing, but he must've read something in her face that warned him not to. With a shrug of his shoulders, he turned back to the gas stove. "Water's boiling."

She put Noah back in his box, much to his protest, and crossed the kitchen. After filling the sink half full with cold water, she stood back for Nick to pour in the hot water. She added dishwashing liquid and began washing.

Nick picked up a towel to dry the dishes after they were rinsed. They worked silently side by side, and Andrea tried to think of some uncontroversial topic of conversation.

"Tell me about your kidnapping in Africa," she finally said.

"There's not much to tell."

"Nick," she protested in disgust. "Surely you aren't so jaded that kidnapping is commonplace in your life."

He growled at her, but she stared at him in challenge.

Finally he said, "No, I guess not. I was riding in a limo, dressed in a business suit, as if we were in New York City, when, as we stopped at a traffic light, three men opened the car doors at once, threw out the other two men with me, pointed a gun at me and sped off. That never happened in New York or Chicago."

"Were the other men Americans also?"

"No. They were with the government there. The kidnappers told me they wouldn't hurt me unless I tried to resist them. Before I knew it, I was dressed in a robe, riding on the back of a camel in the middle of the desert."

"But they didn't hurt you?"

"Not then. When I tried to escape the first time, one of them caught up with me and slugged me on the head with the butt of his rifle."

She couldn't keep from scanning his head, as if looking for blood. "But, Nick, if they weren't going to hurt you, why didn't you just wait for your release?"

"Even if it eventually happened, it might have taken months, even years. Our country has a policy of not giving in to blackmail, and I agree with it."

Strange how a person's feelings about a policy changes when someone they love is involved. Andrea would normally agree with Nick, but the thought of losing him made her a coward.

"So, how did you escape?"

"I found a twelve-year-old who wanted to see America. I promised him a trip to New York City if he'd help me." He gave her an ironic look. "Not everyone rejects my wealth."

"And it was that easy?"

"No. But he could guide me back to the city, and he could get us his uncle's camels without alerting the kidnappers. After that, it was a matter of waiting until the men went to bed. Jahad slipped in and freed me. We had seven hours' head start before they even realized I was gone."

"And you brought him to America?"

"I will. He's safe in the American embassy. Our first priority was finding a decent meal."

"They didn't feed you?" she asked in surprise as she wiped down the sink after finishing the dishes.

"Yeah, but what they considered edible left my stomach in an upheaval. It certainly made me appreciate good food."

"I'm glad things turned out so well," she said, smiling up at him.

He stared at her as if he were looking at something far beyond her. "Yeah." When he continued to stare, she turned away.

"Andy, wait. I—I thought about you a lot while I was tied up."

He seemed to be telling her something, but she wasn't sure what. "I thought about you a lot when I heard you were missing."

"Did you?" he asked, his hand reaching out to caress her cheek. "Did you think what a tragedy it would be if we never shared another kiss, held each other?"

She shivered with longing, but she couldn't give in to his touch. In a tear-laden whisper, she said, "I thought how empty the world would be without you in it."

His lips came down and took hers, bringing all the longing she'd seen in his eyes. His arms wrapped around her, but she didn't give in. Holding still, she waited until he realized she wasn't participating.

When he raised his head and stared at her, she said quietly, "I love you, Nick. I think I've loved you since the day we met. But we don't want the same things. We don't value the same things."

He shoved her away and paced across the room. She watched him, her heart filled with sadness. After several turns around the room, he faced her, his hands on his hips.

"Tell me what you want."

"Tell me about your life. Why do you hold people at bay? What happened to your father? Why don't you ever want a child?"

He answered her last question.

"Can you see me as a father?" His harsh laugh emphasized the incredulity in his voice. "I don't know how to be a father, because my own father was a lousy one."

"Nick, surely—"

"You wanted an answer. There it is. I grew up hating my father. I don't want a kid hating me, blaming me for his problems. The solution is to not have children."

"But, Nick, you don't have to be like your father. You can change. You can—"

"I am like him!" he roared, and began pacing again. "You saw the pictures. But I'm like him in other ways. You ask Bess. She'll tell you I'm like my father."

"But, Nick—"

"You said I was afraid of what I felt for you. Well, you were right. I never let myself care for anyone, because I didn't want to care so much that I lost control of my life. Then you broadsided me. I went down for the count in a matter of seconds. It was as if I had no choice." He took a step toward her and then stopped. "I love you more than life itself. Sitting in that grubby little room in Africa, eating insects to stay alive, all I could think about was finding you."

"Oh, Nick," she said, running across the room to his arms. Her prayers were being answered.

He pulled her tightly against him. "I love you, Andy. If you'll give up this idea of a child, we can be happy. We can have a life together. I'll give you whatever you want...except a child."

It was frightening to go from heaven to hell in seconds. Andrea pressed against him, too weak to pull away, too heartbroken to speak.

"You were right. I started spending less and less time with you while we were married because I was scared of how badly I wanted you, wanted to be with you. I thought if I kept you at a distance I could control what I felt."

Tears oozed from her tightly shut eyes, seeping into

his shirt. What could she say? If she had the choice of not having his child, would she agree to his terms? But she didn't have the choice. His child was already growing in her.

"I realized, when I faced death, that you were too important to let go. We can have a good life, Andy. I'll be whatever you want. We'll travel. I can retire, if necessary. Money's not a problem."

He pulled away from her to see her face. One look into his brilliant blue eyes and she shut hers again.

"Andy?"

"I can't," she whispered, refusing to open her eyes.

"You can't what?"

"I can't promise to give up children."

When he remained silent, holding her, she opened her eyes again and saw the anger building in his.

"You have to have everything your way?" he asked coldly. "I've admitted you were right. I've bared my heart to you. Why can't you be grateful for what we have? Why must you have more?"

"I—I've dreamed of a family, of children, ever since I lost my own. You know my parents were killed in an accident. I lived in foster homes until I was eighteen. They were bad. I mean, they didn't abuse me or mistreat me. But...but I wasn't theirs. I wasn't *family!*" She tore herself from his arms, putting some distance between them.

"I'll be your family, Andy. Bess and I, we can be your family," he urged.

"No," she whispered, turning her back to him,

crossing her arms across her stomach. "No, I want children."

"So you lied."

Shocked, she whirled around. "What? I didn't lie!"

"Yes, you did. You said you loved me. And you accused me of only wanting your body. Well, lady, it sounds like all you want from me is my child."

He stormed from the room, leaving Andrea standing in the center of it, tears streaming down her cheeks.

"No, Nick," she whispered to the empty room. "You're wrong. I already have your child. But I want you, too."

The long, dreary day passed slowly. Andrea made more oatmeal-raisin cookies, to replenish the number they'd eaten since their arrival. She wouldn't want Bess to come home to depleted supplies. And besides, it gave her something to do.

Nick sat in the living room, reading another book. She took him a sandwich for lunch and returned to the kitchen to eat her own in solitude. Noah whimpered a complaint about staying in his box while she ate, after he'd finished his lunch, but she didn't take him out.

Nick was right. She would spoil the puppy and regret it later if she wasn't careful. The same thought occurred to her about her baby. She'd better find some good parenting books to read before she actually had to play the role of mother.

But she knew one thing without any books. She already loved her baby. If, as Nick said, she couldn't have both him and his child, she had to choose the child. Even though she'd love Nick for the rest of her life.

After she cleaned up the kitchen, she found some stationery in Bess's bedroom and brought it back to the kitchen with her. She hadn't yet told Bess about the baby, and she decided to write a letter to her friend and aunt-in-law, explaining everything. It would help her straighten out her head.

Around five that afternoon, the light began to dim, and Andrea realized they'd need to find candles or a lamp before it grew too dark. "Nick?" she called softly from the living room door.

"Yes?"

"We need to find candles or something for light."

Without ever looking up, he said, "Bess keeps candles on the second to the top shelf in the pantry. Don't use more than two or three, in case they have to last us a long time."

His emotionless, practical response irritated her, but she left the room without protesting. After all, she couldn't explain her refusal to give up children. At least, she'd decided she couldn't explain just yet. After they got out of the house, she'd tell him.

But she didn't want to be trapped with Nick Avery when she told him she was already pregnant.

Much to her surprise, Nick appeared in the kitchen a few minutes later. "Shall I fix dinner?"

"There's plenty of meat loaf from last night's dinner, if you don't mind eating leftovers." She kept her eyes trained on his face, but he avoided looking at her.

"I don't mind. It was good meat loaf."

"I'll boil some corn on the cob and make a salad to go with it."

As she stood to begin preparations, he said, "We could just make sandwiches. Meat loaf sandwiches are great."

She grimaced. "That would be good, but unfortunately, we're running out of bread. There are only a couple of slices left, and they're pretty stale."

"Hmm. Do you know how to bake bread?"

For the first time he looked directly at her. She guessed his appetite made her company palatable.

"No. Do you?"

"I remember watching Bess bake it, but it's been a few years. After dinner, we can look at her cookbooks and try to figure it out. I don't want to go without bread."

Andrea doubted either of their abilities to make bread, at least in an edible form, but she wasn't going to argue with Nick. It was a relief to exchange pleasant conversation for a change.

"I'll cut up the salad while you heat the meat loaf and fix the corn," Nick offered, and opened the refrigerator. Though there was no electricity for it and no ice, the temperatures outside and inside were keeping everything reasonably cool. As long as they didn't open it too often.

After he began chopping up lettuce, she asked, "Is the food in the refrigerator okay?"

He shrugged. "The fresh vegetables are all right. I wouldn't want to try the milk. We probably should throw it out."

"All right."

"It's a good thing your puppy is drinking canned milk."

"Yes."

Several more minutes of silence as they worked passed by. "Did you listen to the weather report on the radio?" she finally asked.

"Yeah. It hasn't changed. I noticed the sleet changed to rain for a while this afternoon, but it's back to the frozen stuff now. And I checked the other bedroom. The dripping has finally stopped."

"Oh, good. I didn't know you knew how to fix a roof."

"When you live on a farm, you learn to do most everything."

Such innocuous conversation soothed the raw wounds from their morning fight. She couldn't resist turning the conversation to a more personal topic. "Did you like Homer, Bess's husband?"

A quick look at her and Nick turned his gaze back to the tomato he was slicing. "He was a nice man."

"That's not an enthusiastic endorsement."

"He and Bess married when I was about six. I guess I was jealous of him. And now that I'm older, I realize he was probably jealous of me." With a shrug he added, "He wanted their own children. But Bess never got pregnant."

"But she had you."

"Yeah." He dumped the tomatoes in a bowl with the lettuce and took a bottle of dressing from the refrigerator. Unscrewing the lid, he sniffed and then held the bottle out to Andrea. "Does this smell okay to you?"

"Yes, I think so. The meat loaf and corn won't be ready for about twenty minutes if you want to continue reading." She certainly didn't want him to think she was going to constantly grill him about his past.

"I think I'll search through the cookbooks for a bread recipe. If nothing else, we can make biscuits for breakfast. You do know how to make biscuits?"

She grinned. "Not without a recipe. None of my foster mothers were expert cooks. They knew how to open cans and thaw out meat. When you're cooking in quantity, you don't go in for fancy meals."

Nick gave her a wry look as he pulled down several books from one of Bess's shelves. "Then I'll find a recipe. I consider bread to be a staple, not a luxury."

Much to Andrea's surprise, dinner was pleasant, their conversation casual. Nick talked about what must have been going on in the world the past couple of days, explaining to Andrea how world events affected his business.

Afterward, they located several basic recipes for biscuits and one for bread. Nick even found some yeast in the refrigerator. Andrea promised to try the bread recipe the next day if he agreed to help her.

Just when she was growing panicky because dinner was over and they still had several hours to fill before bedtime, Nick carried a Scrabble game to the table.

"You play Scrabble?" she asked in surprise.

"Bess insisted," he told her dryly.

Whether he played because of Bess or not, she discovered Nick was brilliant at the game, one of her favorites. When he put down the word *xat*, she protested. "Nick, that's not a word. You're just trying to use the *X*."

He raised his eyebrows in a superior fashion. "Feel free to challenge."

"All right, I will." She'd already lost her turn several times and never proven him wrong. But she had nothing to lose this time. She had a *Q*, an *R* and an *L* left and could find nothing to connect them to. Besides, the points from his disputed word would put him over the top. She pulled the dictionary to her.

"Well?" Nick asked with a grin when she found the word.

"Oh, be quiet. How would you know that word? You didn't discuss totem poles all the time, did you?"

"Nope. I studied the dictionary for unusual words so I could win. Homer and I had a competition going the year I was twelve. I didn't mind Bess winning, but I didn't want Homer to best me."

"Well! If I'd known about your expertise, I'm not sure I would've played with you," she exclaimed, but she couldn't help smiling at the picture of a youthful Nick poring over the dictionary.

"It was a good match. You almost beat me."

"Yeah, almost." She stretched and then quickly covered her yawn. A look at her watch showed her it was almost eleven o'clock, much later than she'd thought.

"You're right," Nick said, as if her yawn had been a comment. "It's our bedtime."

The moment she'd been dreading all evening had arrived. She and Nick were going to bed...together.

Chapter Eight

"I need to take a bath," Andrea hurriedly said, not looking at Nick. Anything to delay the moment she had to stretch out beside him. If she took long enough, he might already have fallen asleep.

"No problem. I'll put on some water to heat. While you're bathing, I'll heat more water for me." He stood and began putting his words into action.

"Why don't you bathe first? I need to see to Noah." The puppy had fallen asleep earlier in the evening and she'd tranferred him to his box.

"See to him? He's sleeping."

"I know, but if I wake him now and he takes care of business, maybe he won't have an accident in bed."

"Whose bed?"

Nick's sharp question told her what his reaction would be to her intentions, but she didn't care. Noah was going to be in that bed with the two of them. In fact, he was going to be her chaperon, even if he didn't know it.

"In bed with me. If you don't want us in your bed, we'll return to the couch."

"You're being ridiculous."

"No, I'm not. Noah and I have slept together every night. He'd be frightened if he awoke alone." She walked over to the box and Nick joined her there. They stared at the puppy, curled into a little ball, the faintest sound of snoring rising from him.

"Yeah, he looks like he'd be terrified," Nick commented dryly. "If you insist on having him, go ahead. But you still need to take your bath first."

"Why?"

"So I can carry the heavy pans of water to the bathroom. You're not that big, Andy. I'm afraid you might hurt yourself."

She looked at the four large stew pots already on the burners of the stove and realized he was right. Okay, so she would have to go to bed first. She could pretend to be asleep when he came to bed.

Bending, she shook Noah awake and watched him move around the box.

Nick stood beside her, watching Noah, also. "He is kind of cute, isn't he?" he muttered.

She beamed at him. "You like him, don't you?"

"What's not to like? Except for the accidents, the chewing of the furniture, his constant demand to be held, and eventually, the fleas."

"Noah won't have fleas!" she insisted.

"You're right, he won't. Not if he's sleeping with us." He turned away to look at the stove. "The water's boiling. You'd better get ready for your bath. I'll bring Noah inside in a few minutes."

Andrea hurried out of the kitchen, confusion filling her. Nick had sounded as though he expected them to sleep together in the future, when Noah might have fleas. Did he think their problems had been solved?

Since she knew better, Andrea didn't want to discuss the future with Nick. Not yet. Not until he could leave if he wanted. And he would.

Once she left the kitchen, the temperature dropped considerably. The heat from the candle she carried didn't do much to warm her. She gathered the necessary items quickly and opened the door to the bathroom as Nick came through with the first bucket of water. The four large pots only filled the tub with about two inches of water and she added a little cold water to it. But not much, because the water from the faucet was icy.

She was in and out of the bathwater faster than she'd ever been. By the time she put on clean underwear and the large T-shirt she slept in, she was shivering violently. She left the candle burning for Nick and dashed into the dark bedroom.

Nick had turned down her side of the bed, and she dove under the blankets, pulling them over her. "Nick? I'm out of the bathroom," she called. She hoped he hurried. After protesting their sharing a bed, she was suddenly anxious for him to join her. So she could absorb his warmth and stop shaking.

"Here," Nick said, beside the bed before she even realized he'd come into the room. She reached up for Noah, grateful for even his small warmth. But Nick had a surprise for her.

"Put this at your feet," he suggested and held out an almost flat rubber object.

"What is that?"

"A hot water bottle. It'll warm you up."

He helped her slide it under the covers. The moment her feet touched it, she gasped with pleasure. "Oh, Nick, thank you. I thought I was going to freeze to death."

Grinning, he said, "Just don't use up all the warmth before I can join you." Then he went in the bathroom, and Andrea was left to think about what was to come.

Like Andrea, Nick didn't take long. Wearing Bess's big nightshirt, he scurried around the bed and slid under the covers less than two minutes later.

"That was the fastest bath on record," he muttered.

Andrea could feel him shivering as she had and nudged the hot water bottle toward him. "Here. It's still a little warm."

"So are you," he murmured, and pulled her toward him.

"Nick! Watch out for Noah!" she shrieked as he almost crushed the puppy between them. Noah yelped and began trying to climb Andrea's arm.

"What's the dog doing in the middle of the bed? We need to be close together if we're going to keep each other warm."

"We're close," she insisted. "I—I can feel you." More than was wise. Because the more she felt him, the more she wanted to bury herself in his arms, lose herself in his sexy warmth. And she couldn't do that.

"At least we can share the hot water bottle, Andy," he offered, nudging the rubber bottle back toward her. "Scoot your feet over."

They were both wearing pairs of Homer's socks, since she hadn't brought any socks with her. Feet, encased in socks, shouldn't have been sexy. But then, as far as Andrea was concerned, every inch of Nick was enticing.

He dragged his toes up her calf, straying from the hot water bottle.

"Nick!"

"Mmm-hmm?" he drawled, sounding as if his eyes were closed and he was perfectly innocent.

"Stop that!"

"Sorry. I was just trying to get comfortable."

She considered scooting away from him in protest, but she couldn't bring herself to leave the warmth he provided. She promised herself she'd stay on her guard and make sure Nick didn't take advantage of their situation. If she worked at it, she could stay awake until he slept. After all, it was still early. And that was the last thought she remembered.

She was awakened by a light kiss the next morning.

"Stay in bed. I'll take Noah to the kitchen and start the stove so it will warm up."

Her eyes popped open in time to see Nick disappear into the bathroom. Only seconds later he left the room to go to the kitchen. She'd buried herself under the covers as if she were still asleep, her hand covering her mouth, hoping to fend off the morning sickness until Nick was in the kitchen.

She needed her crackers, but she hadn't wanted to risk them a second time. The first time Nick might not have connected crackers in the morning to the pregnancy, but twice would be stretching it.

As soon as she heard the kitchen door close, she jumped out of bed, closed the bedroom door and then the bathroom door and bent over the toilet, losing her dinner from the night before.

As quickly as possible, she hurried back to the bed, hoping some of their body heat would have lingered in the sheets. Fortunately, Nick didn't open the door until the covers were over her head.

"Andy? I thought I heard you throwing up."

She peeked over the pile of bedding. "I coughed a couple of times. Maybe that's what you heard."

He frowned and came to her side, reaching out to touch her forehead. "You're not getting sick, are you?"

"No. I probably just swallowed the wrong way. I'm fine." She closed her eyes, hoping he'd go away. "Where's Noah?"

"In his box. And complaining at lot. We're going to have to train him not to whine."

Again he talked as if the three of them, Andrea, Noah and him, had a future, and it broke her heart. "It's probably because he's so young. When he gets older, I'm sure he'll behave."

"*I'm* sure he'll do what he wants," Nick said dryly. "He's going to be a big dog." He rubbed his hands up his arms. "I'm heading back to the kitchen. It's a little warmer there. Are you ready for breakfast or do you want to stay in bed awhile?"

"I'll stay in bed for a little longer, if you don't mind," she said, trying to sound sleepy.

He leaned over and kissed her again, taking her by surprise, then left the room.

So much for going back to sleep.

She spent the next hour trying to find a solution to her dilemma. She could go back to Nick and pretend she wasn't pregnant. How long could she hide it from him? If he really loved her, perhaps he wouldn't let her go, even when he finally discovered she was carrying his child.

But she rejected that idea. She wasn't going to lie to Nick. Not telling him *now* wasn't really a lie, she justified to herself. As soon as they were away from here, she would give him the news.

She spent a lot of time fantasizing about Nick's reaction. How she wanted him to be happy, excited, as she was. But even her wildest dreams couldn't conceive such a response. The most she hoped for was a reserved, willing-to-wait-and-see reaction. The worst was a total rejection of her and their child.

She was afraid she knew which one would happen.

When she could bear her thoughts no longer, she left the warmth of the bed and hurriedly dressed before joining Nick in the kitchen.

With the four gas burners turned to their highest

level and the oven lit with the door open, the room offered some warmth. Though not enough to feel comfy. She hurried over to the stove and held out her fingers.

"Don't get too close," Nick warned.

She glared at him. "I'm not an idiot."

"Got up on the wrong side of the bed this morning?" he asked mildly. He was sitting at the table playing solitaire.

"No! I—" she stopped when she realized how useless her anger was. "Sorry. I think I'm frustrated with...with everything."

"Yeah."

"How much longer do you think it will continue?"

"The rain? Or our being stuck here?"

"Either. Both. I don't know. Will they repair the phone lines before the flooding stops?" She turned to stare at first Nick and then the phone on the wall. "Have you checked it lately?"

Before he could answer, she rushed across the room and lifted the receiver. Her hopes crashed as silence greeted her. She jiggled the receiver several times but nothing changed.

She turned around to find Nick watching her. "Yes," he said, "I've checked it."

"I guess you're anxious to be in touch with your office. Did you talk to them before you arrived?"

"Yeah. I called from the plane. Everything is okay at the office, though I told them I'd be back a couple of days ago."

"Maybe they'll institute a search for you," she

suggested, her voice rising in hope. "The police helicopter might return."

"I doubt it. Besides, I'm sure there are others in more desperate situations than us. And it's time for breakfast. Are you cooking?" He deliberately played another card before looking at her.

She didn't want to cook, but she was hungry. "Fine. I'll cook breakfast, but no bacon. How about pancakes?"

"Great. Though I bet Noah would prefer bacon."

He didn't say, like him, but Andrea heard those words in her head. "Well, Noah, can do without this morning. He's already getting fat."

She busied herself with the pancake batter and found the griddle Bess used. When she poured the batter on the griddle for the first pancakes, Nick put the cards away and began setting the table.

"Juice?" he asked as he opened the refrigerator door.

"Yes, please, since we don't have milk."

"I didn't remember you drinking that much milk before," he commented as he filled two juice glasses.

She hadn't been much of a milk drinker, but since she discovered she was pregnant, she'd been making a conscious effort to eat properly. "Um, I think it's good for me."

After they'd eaten breakfast and cleaned up, Andrea felt at loose ends. What should she do now? Nick had an answer.

"I don't suppose you'd be interested in doing some laundry? What little clothes we've found are all dirty.'' Nick was seated at the table shuffling the deck of cards again.

"No, at least not your laundry. But I'll be glad to show *you* how to do it.''

"I was afraid you'd say something like that. I guess living with hired help didn't make this kind of negotiation necessary before.'' He studied her and then said, "How about I build a fire in the living room while you do laundry?''

"How about *I* build the fire and you do *my* laundry?'' she countered, a smile on her face.

"Hmm, no, that's not exactly what I had in mind. Okay, I give. I'll round up my dirty clothes and you can show me how to be a pioneer.'' He shoved his chair back from the table and left the room.

Andrea put water on to boil. Nick was right. They were having to manage, as the pioneers had. At least, in some ways. And they were learning more about each other. Nick was a patient, kind man. He'd make a wonderful father, in spite of his fears.

If he'd only accept that job.

"Andy?''

His reappearance snapped her from her thoughts. "The water's almost ready. You're not washing the overalls, are you?''

"Nope. I figured they'd never get dry. Are you going to do laundry, too?''

"Yes, as soon as you finish.'' She filled the sink half full of cold water, fetched the laundry detergent from the pantry and added a small amount, then reached for the boiling water.

"I'll get it," Nick insisted, and took the water from the stove. "Shall I just pour it in?"

"Yes. Now shake the water around until you make suds and then put the clothes in. If there are any stains, you have to rub the material together. Otherwise, just swish it around."

"Sounds easy enough. But I really am going to have a case of dishpan hands. And I think we'll appreciate Betty's services a little more from now on," he added, referring to the housekeeper.

She excused herself to get her own laundry before he could say anything more about their future. When she got back to the kitchen, she instructed him on rinsing and wringing out the clothes. Then, while he found some rope to make a clothesline between two chairs set far apart in the kitchen, she did her own laundry.

After he finished, Nick went to the living room to build a fire in the fireplace there. He suggested they might wrap themselves in quilts and read by the fire for a change of scenery.

Halfway through the afternoon, when Andrea had dozed off, both Noah and a book in her lap, the puppy suddenly stiffened and began barking.

She snapped awake and reached for her new pet. "Noah? What's wrong?"

Nick put down his book and looked toward the front of the house. "I think Noah smells something." He unwound himself from his quilt and went to the front window.

"What is it?" she asked as she struggled to emerge from the nest she'd made while still holding Noah.

As she started toward the window, a low, ferocious growl startled her. "Was that Noah?" she asked disbelievingly.

"Nope. Some of Noah's relatives have come calling."

"More dogs? Are they puppies?" she asked anxiously, immediately wondering how they would manage to include the new arrivals in their household.

"No, they're not, and we're not letting them in. I think they might have us for dinner if we did."

She reached the window to stand by Nick and look out at the pack of dogs milling around in the front yard. There were five or six of them, some quite large.

The ringleader, on the porch, caught sight of them and began barking loudly. Several other dogs rushed to his side.

"They looked starved to death," she whispered, leaning against Nick.

He looped his arm around her shoulders, pulling her closer. "They probably are, but if we feed them, they won't go away."

"But I feel so sorry for them."

"Andy, the floods are hard on everyone. You've rescued Noah, but that's about all we can do. These fellows are big enough to take care of themselves." He glanced down at the puppy in Andrea's arms. "Besides, Noah doesn't seem too happy with our guests. With good reason. They'd eat him for dinner, too."

She leaned her head against his broad shoulder and his other arm came around her, putting her wholly into his embrace. A nice place. "I guess you're right. When will they go away?"

"Maybe not until dark. So don't even think of venturing out onto the porch, okay?"

"Okay," she agreed with a big sigh.

"Is that such a sacrifice?"

"No, of course not. But I think I'm getting a bad case of cabin fever. How far is it to Bess's neighbors?"

"The nearest neighbor is about two miles, but he's the one who took her to the hospital. I'm not sure he made it back to his place. The next one is over five miles away, in the opposite direction."

"Maybe we should walk to their house tomorrow. We could use their telephone, get some help."

"Assuming their telephone worked. And if it didn't, we'd face another five-mile walk back, or staying there with strangers. And they might not have the food and warmth we've got." He tightened his hold on her. "Not a good idea, Andy. I know you're frustrated, but we're better off staying put until the telephone lines are connected up again."

"I guess so." Her forlorn tones must have provoked Nick because he shook her lightly.

"Hey, I can assure you I'm right. After all, compared to what I just lived through in Africa, I'm in a palace. And the food is better than what the best *cordon bleu* chef could produce in Paris in comparison." He lowered his voice and whispered in her ear,

"And the company is my first pick, no matter where I am."

She managed a shaky smile, turning to thank him, and his lips met hers. He spun her around to face him and deepened the kiss, stirring fires within her. It was Noah licking his face that caused Nick to break off the kiss.

"When we get back to Chicago, that dog is going to have to entertain himself every once in a while and leave us alone," he growled before kissing her again, this time a light caress that left her wanting more. "Do you think he'll learn to live in the apartment, or should we look for a place with a yard?"

Andrea bit her bottom lip, unsure how to answer. If she was truthful, Nick would be angry. Their peaceful existence since yesterday afternoon had been wonderful. But she couldn't let him believe they were going to live together. After a deep sigh, she turned her head away, leaning against his chest, and said quietly, "Noah and I aren't going back to Chicago."

He froze, his hands stilling on her body. Then he jerked her back so he could see her face. "What did you say?"

"I never said Noah and I were going to…to live with you in Chicago, Nick. You just assumed—"

His blue eyes were fierce, his frown heavy, as he stared at her. "But I told you I'd give you what you wanted! I agreed to change! I'll talk about whatever you want, Andy. We're made for each other!"

She kept her gaze fastened on his chest but she shook her head no.

"Look at me, damn it! Tell me what's wrong!"

Finally she did as he asked. Staring at his beloved face, she whispered, "I told you. I can't give up having children, Nick. And I never will."

Chapter Nine

She watched the anger rise in Nick, his eyes narrowing, his lips thinning, as he reacted to her words.

"So, no compromise, no trying to work things out. You have to have everything your way, no matter what?"

"No, no compromise," she said quietly, turning back to the window. "I told you about my growing up in the foster homes, dreaming of one day having my own family again. That's not a dream I will abandon."

"*I'm* your family," Nick said forcefully, stepping forward to catch her shoulders. "Bess and I are your family. You don't have to have children to justify your existence or to have family. I know some women feel that way, but you shouldn't, Andy."

His voice was low, caressing, and she loved the sound of it. But she shook her head no.

"What if I were sterile?" he demanded, his voice losing its caressing tones. "Or had had an operation? What then?"

"But you aren't."

"How do you know? I never intend to have children, so why not have an operation?"

She had to be careful, or he would know she was pregnant. Then the days until their rescue would be intolerable. "Have you had an operation? And if you have, don't you think you should have told me before you married me?" she asked, twisting in his hold.

He dropped his hands from her shoulders and took a step back from her. "Why? Did you tell me a prerequisite for your staying married to me was having children?"

He had a good point. The only difficulty was that she had been so entranced, so overwhelmed by his dynamic presence, she hadn't thought to ask about anything. She'd just assumed he, too, would want a family. "No."

"Then you weren't honest with me, either."

"I didn't attempt to purposely deceive you," she pointed out, glaring at him. "If you've had an operation, then you did deceive me." How bizarre. They were arguing about something she knew wasn't true.

He turned away from her. "I haven't had an operation, but I've thought about it."

She said nothing. What could she say? *I know. I'm glad. I'm pregnant.* No, she couldn't say those things.

Facing her again, he asked, "So, you're telling me

you won't come back to me, won't continue our marriage unless I agree to children?''

She nodded her head.

''But you love me?''

She nodded again.

He put his hands on his hips and began pacing the room, a favorite occupation when he was thinking. When he came to a stop in front of her, she braced herself. She could tell by the look in his eyes that he thought he'd found a way out.

''Look, we've invested six months into our marriage already. Why don't we give it another year? Try making our marriage work? I'll admit I was…was less than cooperative the last couple of months.'' He offered her a charming, boyish smile that had always served him well. ''I was afraid, just like you said. The only person I'd ever loved and trusted was Bess. It was scary. But I understand myself better. I'm willing to trust you. So, we'll give the marriage another year, and then we'll discuss the future.''

So reasonable. So positive. So impossible.

He stood there, the epitome of every woman's dream. Rich, charming, caring, handsome. She couldn't think of anything to object to, except for one thing. And, as of two months ago, that one thing was non-negotiable.

''Well?'' he prompted, his smile still in place.

She could lie to him, tell him she'd think about her decision. But she wanted to be honest. To a point.

''No,'' she whispered, meeting his confident look and then turning away.

A pulsing silence filled the room. She had no idea what to expect. When he finally spoke, the controlled rage that filled his voice frightened her.

"Why didn't you tell me?"

She stared at him, fear filling her. "What?" she whispered, wide-eyed.

"There can be only one reason for turning me down, Andrea, my sweet, and I don't think you've been playing fair," he intoned.

Her heart ached. He'd figured out her secret, and his anger was greater than she'd thought it would be. "Nick, I promise I was going to—"

"To tell me? How kind of you. And *when* were you going to tell me? After you'd put me through the emotional wringer, made me realize what I would be losing? How torturous of you, my dear. I wouldn't have thought you were such a vengeful woman." His scorn lacerated her heart. She hadn't expected him to take it quite so hard. After all, she wasn't trying to entrap him.

"Look, Nick, I'm not forcing you—"

"Who is he?" His sharp question, as if he'd reached the end of his patience, shocked her.

When she didn't answer, he grabbed her shoulders again and shook her lightly. "Who is he, damn it? Not someone who works for me?"

"What are you talking about?" She was bewildered by his questions.

"Who's the man taking my place? The father of those future children you want so badly." When she stared at him, in shock, he repeated, "Is it someone who works for me? Because if it is, he'll be out of a job so fast it will make your head spin. Then how will you pay for all those children?"

"No. No, it's not anyone who works for you." She tried to think, to decide how to handle his wild accusations, but her head was filled with his anger.

"So, it's someone in Kansas City. Fast work, Andrea," he snarled. But he turned loose of her shoulders and took another turn about the room. "Is he rich?"

She closed her eyes. "My life now is none of your business."

"You're still my wife," he reminded her, his voice even, devoid of emotion.

She cuddled Noah against her, suddenly feeling cold, colder than she had all day. Only the puppy's warmth seemed real.

"Are you already sleeping with him? Working on those children you're determined to have?" Nick continued, as if she had responded to his previous insults.

Andrea stared at him, pain in her eyes. How could he believe she would want any other man after the six months they'd spent together? She'd left him, yes, but only because he was withdrawing. Because there wasn't enough of him! And because of the baby.

"You're insane! There's no one," she said, her voice shaking with emotion.

"Took you a while to deny it, didn't it, Andrea. What's wrong? Afraid it will affect your divorce settlement?" His voice was growing tighter, harder, if that were possible, with each verbal punch.

Tears filled her eyes, but she fought to contain them. She wasn't going to let him know how badly he'd hurt her with his accusations. Clutching Noah to her chest, she headed for the door.

"Where are you going?" he demanded.

"Where you aren't," she snapped.

Unfortunately, she didn't have too many choices.

Andrea paced the kitchen for almost half an hour before she figured out how to relieve her stress and anger. Bread. They'd talked the day before about making bread, but then they'd forgotten it with the loss of electricity.

At least making bread would keep her from thinking about the argument she and Nick had just had. And from strangling him.

She opened the pantry and took out the cookbook that Nick had found the night before. After reading the instructions for making bread, she looked at her watch. It was almost three o'clock. The bread probably wouldn't be ready until eight, but she wasn't in any hurry. After all, where did she have to go?

The recipe called for milk. She'd have to substitute canned milk, maybe mixed with a little water, she decided. Not a gourmet cook, she wasn't sure that would work, but Nick wouldn't dare complain if the results weren't perfect. At least, he'd better not.

She pulled the yeast Nick had located from Bess's refrigerator and began her preparations. Half an hour later, she was kneading the dough with great force, enjoying the physical punishment she could mete out without any retribution. With regret, she finally realized she had to stop.

Covering the bowl in which she'd placed the dough, she put it on a shelf over the stove, sure that would be the warmest location in the kitchen. Now what? She had to let it rise for an hour and a half before she could punch it again.

At that moment, the door swung open and Nick walked in. She glared at him, letting him know he was invading her territory. "What do you want?"

"I was going to get the radio so I could listen to the weather report." He turned away, but something made him face her again, a frown on his face. "What are you doing?"

"Nothing." She wasn't about to tell him of her attempt to make bread.

"You have a streak of flour on your cheek. You're cooking something?"

"What I do is none of your business," she assured him, her nose in the air, even as she tried to wipe her face clean.

With abrupt movements, he picked up the radio. Then he faced her again, his lips pressed tightly together. "Look, Andrea, we still have to share this house until something can be arranged. If you refuse to cook for me, I'll manage. But I think it's a little childish."

"I didn't say I would refuse to cook for you. You've certainly cooked for me the past couple of days. I'm willing to be reasonable about things like that." It took a lot of control to sound so rational.

She felt it slip a little. "But I don't want to *chat* with someone who accused me of...of—" She couldn't bring herself to say the word.

He had no such difficulty. "Adultery? Is that the word you're looking for?"

"Yes," she stormed. "Adultery."

"If the shoe fits..." he suggested, with a hard look.

"It doesn't fit. I would never betray you or my promises in such a way. But the fact that you would even suggest such a thing tells me you don't know me."

Much to her surprise, he backed down. "Look, I apologize. Maybe you haven't slept with him yet, but I don't think it was fair for you to jerk my chain when you already had a replacement lined up."

"Nick, I swear—"

"Don't, Andy. Just don't. It hurts too much." Without another word, he took the radio and left the room.

Did he think she wasn't hurting? Did he think leaving him was easy? Or enjoyable? The past month she'd suffered every night as she'd crawled into her lonely bed, every morning when she'd woken up alone...and frequently sick. And living without Nick would hurt the rest of her life.

She put on water to make a cup of tea. It would give her something to do until she could punch the bread dough again.

She put the bread in the oven to bake at a little after seven. All afternoon she'd alternated sessions of pummeling the dough with industrious cleaning or silent debate.

She'd heard nothing else from Nick.

Next time she decided to avoid the man, she would take the living room and he could have the kitchen. Then he could cook, and she would lie around all day reading.

But then who would take care of Noah? With his box located in the kitchen, she needed to be nearby. She tiptoed over to peer down into the box. After a warm milk dinner, he was curled up sleeping again.

If only life were so simple.

The door swung open and Nick came in.

"Are you planning dinner anytime soon, or should I fend for myself?"

"I thought I'd fry some chicken. Would you peel potatoes to go with it?" she asked coolly.

He gave her a stern look, but answered politely. "Yes, of course."

Taking a pan and the bag of potatoes she handed him, he got a knife from one of the drawers and sat at the table. After a moment of silence he said, "Something smells good."

"I'm baking bread."

"I thought you didn't know how," he commented, frowning.

"I learned."

She began flouring the pieces of chicken she'd cut up. Then she took a large skillet and heated oil in it. Just as she dropped the first piece of chicken in the hot oil, Nick spoke again.

"It's supposed to warm up tomorrow."

"Good."

"I'll walk to the neighbors."

She almost dropped the next piece of chicken on the floor. "What did you say?"

"As soon as I'm sure it's going to warm up and you'll be all right by yourself, I'm going to walk to the neighbors. If their phone isn't working, maybe they'll have a car and will either loan it to me or drive me into town." He kept his gaze on the potato he was peeling.

"What about those dogs? Won't they attack you?" Her voice trembled at the thought.

"They're probably gone. But I'll find a stout stick to take with me."

"Nick, I don't think this is a good idea." She tried to concentrate on the chicken, but she kept seeing visions of Nick being attacked by the dogs. "It's too dangerous."

"I'll be fine." He finished one potato and reached for another. "How many shall I peel?"

How could he worry about such mundane things as potatoes when he was talking about risking his life the next day? She tried to think up a reason to keep him with her. "I'll be frightened here alone."

"How many potatoes?"

"Four. Did you hear me? I don't want you to go. I'll be scared."

"If you stay inside and keep the doors locked, you'll be fine." He continued to peel the potatoes.

Andrea put the rest of the chicken in the skillet and

covered it. "Why have you decided to go now? Earlier you said it wasn't a good idea."

"You know why, Andy," he said, finally meeting her gaze. "We can't go on like this."

Tears formed again. "Like what? We spent the afternoon all right. What difference does it make if we stay in different rooms, as long as we're both safe?"

He sighed as he put down the potato he'd finished peeling and picked up another one. "I'm not a patient man, Andy. A slow death never appealed to me. That's why I escaped the kidnappers. If I was going to die, I wanted it to happen then, not a year later after living in miserable conditions."

"You're comparing the conditions here to Africa?" she demanded, her voice rising. "You're saying our...our argument is a slow death? Nick, you're being ridiculous!"

He didn't respond.

She couldn't think of anything else to say. Lifting the lid off the skillet, she turned the chicken. Then, after putting the lid back in place, she turned to face him. "Okay. Noah and I will go with you."

That got his attention. He looked at her with a frown. "You'll do no such thing."

"How will you stop me? And if you have the right to risk your life, then I do, too."

"Be serious, Andy. It's five miles in thick mud. You'd be exhausted by the time we got to the end of Bess's driveway."

He could be right, she realized. Her energy level

was much lower since the pregnancy. But she wasn't going to admit that to Nick. "I'll make it."

"For what purpose? It won't take two of us to use the phone. If I catch a ride into town, I can rent a car by myself."

"What good would that do? You said the bridge was out on the only road above water to Bess's house," she noted.

"Okay, I'll rent a helicopter. I'll get you out, I promise. And we'll end this tête-à-tête."

"I want to come with you."

"No."

"Nick—"

"Is the chicken burning? I smell something burning."

She jerked the lid off the skillet, but the chicken was turning a nice shade of brown, not black. Then she opened the oven to check on the two loaves of bread. "Nothing's burning. I want—"

"Let's wait until after dinner. I can't argue on an empty stomach." He stood and carried the four peeled potatoes over to the sink to wash them. Then he cut them up and put them into the pan, filled it with water and placed it on a burner.

"Where's the salt?" he asked.

She handed it to him silently, frustration filling her. Was he using delaying tactics? Did he think he could distract her and she'd forget their argument, as if she were a child?

The rest of the preparations for dinner were done in silence. She fixed a salad while the potatoes and chicken were cooking, and Nick set the table. Then he made a pot of coffee.

When the loaves of bread came out of the oven, the entire kitchen was filled with the heavenly smell of warm bread. "We need to let it cool a few minutes before we try to slice it," she said.

"Let me set them in the hallway. It won't take long away from the stove." He lifted the two pans with hot pads and walked out the door.

While he was gone, she put the food on the table.

"Five minutes ought to have them stone cold," he assured her with a shiver as he came back through the door.

"Do you want to eat now or wait for the bread?"

"Let's wait. The bread smells great. I had no idea you could bake bread." He gave her a social smile, stiff and formal.

Short of twiddling their thumbs, they had nothing to do. Finally she asked, "Did you hear any news when you listened to the weather earlier?"

"A few headlines, nothing important. I guess if we didn't have the radio, we could be the last two people on earth and not know it."

"I guess so." Silence fell again, and Andrea hated the tension. She jumped up. "I think the bread is ready."

It was a silent meal; each of them kept their gazes on their plates. At least, Andrea assumed that's what Nick did. She didn't look at him so she couldn't be sure.

Afterward, they politely cleaned the dishes together, acting as if they'd just met.

"Well, I'll look forward to breakfast in the morning knowing we'll have your delicious bread to eat." He smiled his fake smile again.

"Stop it, Nick!"

"What do you mean?"

"Stop pretending that everything is okay. Stop pretending that we don't have a discussion to finish."

He gave her a wry smile, but at least it was genuine. "Discussion is a nice term for what we were having."

"All right, argument. But it's not going to go away just because you ignore it." She crossed her arms and stared at him.

"Andy, you can't go with me. You'd only make the trip more dangerous for me."

"Aha! So you admit it could be dangerous!"

"With you along, it would be," he said coolly, leaning against the cabinet, his hands in his pockets.

"What about those dogs? If they see you, I think they'd be more afraid of two people than one."

"You could be right. But I'd be so concerned with protecting you, I couldn't climb a tree or run away. Then we'd both be in trouble."

Drat him! He sounded so reasonable. But she couldn't let him go. She gnawed her bottom lip, thinking. Finally she raised her head and looked at him. "Will you explain something to me?"

"Sure. But I promise I'll be careful, and I'll come

back for you. What else is there to explain?'' He had relaxed, thinking he'd won this battle.

"Explain to me again why you won't have any children.''

Chapter Ten

"What does my not wanting children have to do with anything? We're discussing my walking to a neighbor's house," Nick complained, frowning.

Andrea moved to the table and sat again. She wanted him to know she wasn't going anywhere until she got some answers. "I may not see you again. I'd like to really understand why you are so adamant about kids."

"Come on, Andy, you won't even consider staying married to me. It's a moot point." He was jingling something in his pockets, telling Andrea he was nervous.

"Surely, Nick, I deserve an explanation. After all, your decision affects me."

"You didn't explain until now why having a child is so important to you. And that decision affects me," he pointed out, his lips set in stubborn lines.

"We should have discussed a lot before we married. But everything happened so fast. But I can't change how I feel just because it doesn't fit your idea of the future. I missed the feeling, the connection of family. I want it back again."

"And I already told you Bess and I would be your family. You don't need kids."

"I do need a child. I want to be a mother. You know I love Bess…and you." She hated telling him of her love after the things he'd accused her of, but it was the truth. "That's not the same thing as being a mother."

"Then be a mother," he growled, "but leave me out of it."

He pushed away from the counter and started toward the door.

"Wait!" Andrea called, finding it difficult to believe he thought he could just walk away. "You haven't explained again why you object to children."

"It's late, Andy. I'm tired."

"Bull! You're avoiding opening up. Remember how you promised you'd talk more, spend more time with me?"

"That was before you refused to come back to me," he snapped. "If there's no future for us, what the hell difference does it make?"

"I need to know, Nick," she said quietly, her eyes pleading as much as her words. "Is it because your mother died giving birth to you?"

He stood there, his hands on his hips, his head

down, and Andrea held her breath, waiting for him to make the next move.

Suddenly, he lifted his head and his blue eyes pinned her in place. "Isn't that reason enough? Do you know how devastated I'd be if I got you pregnant and it killed you?"

"Nick, medicine has made great strides. Besides, in my family, no one has ever died from childbirth." At least she didn't think so.

"My head hears you. My heart doesn't." He walked slowly to her side and reached out to cup her cheek. "I can do without a child if it means endangering your life."

"But that's not your only reason, is it?" She knew it wasn't. Somehow she knew his remarks about his father were a part of it, as he'd said earlier.

He shrugged a shoulder and turned away.

"Nick?" she prodded.

"You just won't leave it alone, will you, Andy? What do you want to do? Learn every one of my little secrets?" He paused and blew out a gust of air. "Well, here's my deep, dark secret. I never speak of my life, of my father because he was an alcoholic."

"Nick, lots of people deal with—"

"And he hated me."

"No! He couldn't—"

"Not a pretty picture, is it? My father hated my guts because he blamed me for my mother's death. He took every opportunity to let me know it, too." His gaze was hard as he stared across the kitchen, as if seeing scenes from his childhood.

She reached out and touched his arm, needing to connect with him, to pull him back to the present. "Nick, I'm sorry. It must've been horrible. But why would that stop you from having a child?"

He slowly turned to look at her, and a mocking smile appeared on his lips. "Because I'm just like the bastard."

She was stunned by his vehemence. "What are you saying? You're not…not like that."

"Yes, I am."

"But you don't drink. I've never seen you drink."

"Nope. Because I learned early what it would do to me. I got pulled over by a local cop when I was a teenager. I'd really tied one on. While he was hauling me in, that policeman said the one thing that made me stop drinking."

"What?"

"Like father, like son."

She gasped, watching the impact those words had on a teenage boy all over again on Nick's face.

A steely determination filled his gaze as he turned it back to her. "Those words are stamped on my brain."

"But, Nick, if you can overcome something as difficult as drinking, being a father would be a cinch." Her heart was burgeoning with hope.

"No."

"But, Nick—"

"No, Andy. I can't risk it. I'd be condemned to hell and I'd take my child with me. I promised myself I'd never take that step. And I won't." He pulled himself together and moved away. "Now you know. And I don't ever want to discuss it again. If you want to come back on my terms, I'd...I'd love you forever," he finished in a whisper. "If not..." He paused before a wry smile, full of pain, filled his face. "I'll still love you forever. But I won't be married to you."

Before she could think of anything to say to his heartbreaking statement, he walked out of the kitchen.

She put her head down on her folded arms and allowed the tears she'd held back to fall.

An hour later Andrea was still seated at the table but she'd stopped crying long ago. Her marriage was over. She'd finally accepted that. Except she still had to do one thing.

She had to tell Nick she was pregnant.

But not tonight. She couldn't tell him she was pregnant and then crawl into bed to sleep beside him.

Tomorrow, however, before he left her, she would tell him. He had to know before he set out on his walk.

She rubbed her face, exhausted. Her mental workout was much more tiring than any physical exercise. Standing, she was surprised to discover how stiff her muscles felt. Relaxing in a tub of steaming hot water would've helped, but that wasn't possible. She filled the four pots they'd used the night before to heat water and put them on the stove. At least she could have a little hot water.

When the water was ready, she lifted the first off

the stove and wondered how she'd ever get it to the bathroom. By the time she reached the hallway, her arms were trembling. When Nick silently appeared and took the pot away from her, she didn't protest.

They didn't exchange any words, however. They'd already said everything that had to be said.

She bathed quickly and returned to the kitchen to fetch Noah. Nick was sitting at the table.

"I'm out of the bath," she said, knowing her statement was unnecessary, but she didn't know what else to say.

"Thanks. I just filled the hot water bottle if you want to take it with you."

"Thank you." Brilliant dialogue. She took the rubber bottle from the table, scooped up Noah, and fled the kitchen.

Nick didn't come to bed right away, and Andrea tried to relax, to clear her mind of the misery of the evening. She must have finally succeeded, because she fell asleep before Nick arrived.

Sometime during the night she awakened to the feeling of a strong arm encircling her, shifting her slightly against Nick's warm body. She came awake enough to wonder about Noah, but the warm ball on her other side told her he was safe.

And she was safe, too, in Nick's arms…for one more night. She couldn't have moved away, for any reason. She wanted this one last time in Nick's embrace.

When Nick awoke the next morning his shifting in the bed awakened Andrea. She grabbed the side of the bed as if it were a raft in the ocean. As Nick rolled to the other side of the bed and swung his legs to the floor, she felt her stomach heave in protest.

"Oh, no!" she moaned, and shoved back the cover. With no thought to her audience, she ran for the bathroom.

"Andy? Andy, are you all right?" Nick called from behind her.

Her goal was the toilet and she hung over it as her insides emptied with great thoroughness. In the midst of her misery, she felt Nick's warm hand hold her head as the other held her against him, lending support.

Several miserable minutes later he grabbed a nearby cloth and wiped her face for her, then lifted her to her feet and carried her back to bed. Which was a good thing, Andrea thought. As much as she was trembling, she'd never have made the return trip.

After tenderly tucking the covers around her, he felt her face. "You're not running any fever," he commented, a puzzled tone in his voice. "Do you think you caught a virus?"

She groaned in response, unwilling to explain anything until she'd recovered. He left her in blessed peace and she didn't bother asking why. Closing her eyes, she sank into a tired lethargy that might have led to a return to sleep had Nick not come back.

"Do you want a drink of water?"

"No," she muttered, keeping her eyes closed.

"I found a can of soda. That might help settle your stomach. Would you drink some of that?"

"I need to sleep."

"Drink a little soda first," he urged. "I want to be sure you can keep something down."

He slipped his arm beneath her shoulders and lifted her slightly. She opened her eyes to discover the can of soda at her mouth. After sipping a little of the liquid, she turned her head away.

"That's enough," she whispered. Suddenly she remembered a yelp from Noah as she was rushing to the bathroom. "Noah?"

"He's okay. Just a quick tumble to the floor. You want him back in bed with you?" Nick asked.

"No, take him to the kitchen," she said, already closing her eyes.

"Do you want any breakfast? I could try to make something light."

"No, just sleep. That's all I want."

She felt his gaze on her, but he remained silent. Slowly she drifted off.

When she came to, she was alone. And her stomach felt fine, much to her relief. Fully awake at last, she looked at her watch. It was almost eleven o'clock. She remembered Nick's plan to walk to a neighbor's. Had he already left?

She wished that Nick would be gone so she wouldn't have to tell him about the baby, but she discarded such thoughts at once. He had to know.

Finally, after last night, she understood that he wouldn't want anything to do with the baby...or her.

He had too many demons from the past to fight. But she had to tell him about his child.

She pushed back the covers, more sedately this time, and went to the bathroom to dress. Halfway there, she realized the rooms were no longer icy. The cold front must have disintegrated. But it hadn't taken away the rain. She could still hear it hitting the windows.

When she reached the kitchen, she found it empty. Hurrying to Noah's box, she discovered it, too, had no occupant. He couldn't have taken Noah with him?

She rushed to the living room and breathed a sigh of relief to discover Nick reclining on the couch reading a book. Her relief changed to amusement as she noted Noah curled up on his chest, enjoying Nick's rhythmic stroking.

"I'm glad you two are friends," she said softly, enjoying Nick's sudden scramble to sit up. Noah immediately protested his movement and then began wagging his tail and barking at Andrea.

"Are you all right? You've slept a long time," Nick said as he stood and walked to her side.

"I'm fine."

He felt her forehead again. "Still no fever? How's the stomach?"

"Empty. I'm starving."

"I don't think you should eat much, Andy. Maybe a little soup." He took her by the arm and led her to the sofa. "You rest here and I'll heat up some soup and bring it to you."

She meekly did as he said, even though she

would've preferred a steak to soup. "Could I have some crackers with the soup?"

"Sure."

"How about a grilled cheese sandwich?"

"No. You can't have dairy products on an upset stomach." He didn't wait for a response.

Noah jumped up at her, his paws clawing her legs. "Okay, okay, Noah," she responded, picking him up. "But you really are getting spoiled."

At least, after she told Nick of her pregnancy, she could eat what she wanted. Soup would keep her going for a little while. She crossed to the window to stare out at the rain. It was almost gentle now, a heavy mist, rather than a downpour, but it was still coming down.

Nick would be drenched if he walked out, but at least it wasn't as cold, though the fire felt good. How long would it take him to make the walk? Would he reach the neighbor's by nightfall? Or would he wait until tomorrow to start?

"Oh, dear," she whispered. What if she told him she was pregnant and he couldn't leave today? They would have to spend another twenty-four hours staring at each other, not speaking.

The door opened to admit Nick, carrying a tray. The smell of chicken noodle soup erased all her questions. Her hunger dominated all her thoughts.

"Oh, thank you. I'm starving," she said as she sat on the sofa exchanging Noah for the tray.

"You'd best take it slowly, see if it stays down," he cautioned, watching her with an eagle eye.

She tried to go slowly, to appease him, but she finished the bowl quickly. "Is there any more?"

"Yes, but I'm not sure—"

"Please?"

He took the bowl from her and left the room without speaking. Returning with more soup and crackers, he again watched her eat.

"That was wonderful. Thanks."

"No queasiness? You're not going to throw up again?"

She noticed he kept his distance, as if afraid he'd be in the line of fire if she suddenly got sick again. "No, I'm fine."

"Good."

"Uh, Nick, are you still going to walk out today?"

"And leave you here alone, sick? Of course not. We'll wait and see how you feel in the morning."

She almost groaned. She knew how she'd feel in the morning. The same way she'd felt every morning for the past six weeks. And the doctor had told her it could possibly last for another month.

"How long will it take you to walk to the neighbor's?"

He shrugged. "It's about five miles straight across the fields, but more like eight miles by road. But I think it will be safer and faster by road, so maybe two or three hours."

"Oh, then you could still go today."

He stared at her, a frown on his face. "I thought you didn't want me to go. Why the sudden change?"

Andrea licked her suddenly dry lips. "You seemed

determined to go. I didn't think I could change your mind.''

"Well, you did. I'm not going off and leaving you here sick.''

Should she tell him now? "Nick, I'm sure—''

"No, Andy. I might not be able to get back until tomorrow. If you threw up the rest of the day like you did this morning, you might get dehydrated. It wouldn't be safe to leave you alone.''

"Nick, I won't get dehydrated because—''

"Quit being so stubborn! First you don't want me to go. Then you want me to go. I have to do what I think is best.'' He folded his arms over his chest and glared at her.

He wasn't in the best of moods to hear her secret, but she had to tell him now, while there was still time for him to make the hike. And she knew her news would send him out into the storm. He wouldn't want to hang around once he found out what had made her throw up.

"I have something to tell you, Nick.'' She stood, even though her knees were shaking as much as her voice.

"Sit back down before you fall over, Andy. You're trembling like a leaf.'' He walked to her side and gently pushed her back to the sofa.

"I'm fine,'' she muttered, watching his face. This revelation was going to be so difficult. She probably would never see him again once he left. She took a deep breath and closed her eyes.

"I think you need to be back in bed," Nick said, and bent to scoop her up in his arms.

"No! No, I have to tell you something," she protested, pushing his hands away.

He squatted beside her, bringing his blue eyes level with hers. "Okay," he agreed softly, as if talking to a frightened child, "tell me whatever it is that's so important, and *then* you can go back to bed."

Nodding, she opened her mouth to reveal the one thing her husband didn't want to hear...and the phone rang.

Chapter Eleven

They didn't move for several more rings, staring at each other in shock. Then, Nick cried hoarsely, "The phone!" and ran for the kitchen.

Andrea wasn't far behind him. She really hadn't believed the service would be restored until the rain had stopped, which wasn't expected anytime soon.

"Hello?" Nick gasped into the phone. "Yes. Yes, we're here. But we need a helicopter to come get us out."

It was over. Their ordeal was over, Andrea thought with a sigh filled with both relief and regret. Regret because her time with Nick was almost gone. She crossed the kitchen to put Noah, still in her arms, in his box.

"Of course it's an emergency!"

Her attention was jerked back to Nick's conversation. What did he mean? Why—

"My wife is ill. If she keeps throwing up, she'll become dehydrated and I don't know what to do to help her," he insisted, his voice hard.

She hurried to his side. "No! No, wait, Nick. That's not true."

He gave her a funny look, but didn't ask any questions. Obviously he was listening intently to whoever was speaking.

"Nick, listen to me. I won't throw up again."

He covered the receiver with his hand. "You can't know that, Andy, and I don't want to take any chances with you."

Was he thinking of his mother? Had she not gotten medical help in time? Andrea couldn't leave him in ignorance.

"Nick, I'm not sick. I'm pregnant."

He stared at her, his face paling in an alarming fashion. No longer aware of the phone in his hand, he let the receiver fall.

"Sit down before you pass out," she ordered, feeling a surge of adrenaline. Or maybe it was relief that she'd finally confessed. Picking up the receiver from where it dangled by the cord, she spoke into the phone. "Hello?"

"Ma'am, is this Mrs. Avery?"

"Yes."

"Your husband said—"

"I'm fine, but we'd like to get out of here."

"If no one's in danger there, we have other people who need our help. Your aunt, Bess Avery, has been bugging us to find out what happened to the two of you. Since you have a phone, could you call her, please?''

''Yes, of course. Is she still at the hospital?''

''No. Here's the number she gave us.''

After she'd written down the number, she asked the most important question. ''When will you be able to come get us out?''

''I don't know, ma'am,'' that harried impersonal voice said. ''We'll come as soon as possible.''

Her thank-you was ignored and the connection clicked off before she finished speaking. Hanging up the receiver, she turned to face her husband.

He was staring at her with a mixture of pain and anger, but she was relieved to see his color had improved.

''Nick, they can't—''

''How can you be pregnant?'' he asked, spitting out the last word as if it were dirty.

''The—the normal way,'' she replied, chewing on her bottom lip.

''You know what I mean. I used protection!''

''The only completely safe birth control is abstinence, Nick, and we certainly didn't practice that.''

''Are you sure—''

''Don't even ask that question, Nicholas Avery,'' she warned, anger boiling up in her.

He buried his face in his hands, but at least he didn't pursue the question of paternity. Andrea hoped his silence meant he knew he was the father.

''Nick, they don't know when they can come for

us. It could be several days. Is there any way to arrange something? Is there someone you can call?''

He didn't move and she wondered if he'd heard her questions. Something had to be done before the phone went dead again.

''Nick?''

This time he stood, but he avoided looking at her. ''Yeah.'' He reached for the phone and she moved aside.

He rapidly punched in a lot of numbers. Then, jerkily, as if he'd received a physical blow, he barked into the phone, giving someone instructions for hiring a helicopter to come pick them up.

When he hung up the receiver, he leaned against the wall, his forehead resting on the blue-flowered wallpaper, saying nothing.

''Nick? When will they come?''

''I don't know. They'll call.''

''Who? Who will call?''

''My office. As soon as they can arrange something.''

After the excitement of the past few minutes, Andrea felt strangely limp. What did she do now? ''I—I should begin cleaning. I don't want to leave Bess's house a mess.''

''Wait!'' Nick called roughly, straightening from the wall.

She stopped and slowly turned to face him. The sinking feeling in her stomach matched the look on his face. ''Yes?''

''When did you find out?''

No need to ask his meaning. "The day before I left you."

His gaze burned into her. "Is the baby the reason you left?"

She took a deep breath. "Yes. You told me twice you'd never have a child. When I discovered I was pregnant, I couldn't stay. My child will be loved," she ended fiercely.

"So you understand how impossible it would be for me to be a father?"

She took a step closer to him. "You will be a father whether you acknowledge my baby or not. What you do about your role as father is up to you."

"Andy, there are other ways—"

"No! Don't even say the words. I will have my child, alone if necessary. Nothing and no one will stop me." She threw her shoulders back, as if facing a firing squad. In truth, she was preparing herself to hear his rejection.

"I can't be a part of this," he said dully, his gaze drifting from her face to the wall behind her.

As much as she loved him, she wasn't sure she could ever forgive him for that rejection of her baby. Her precious baby. "Don't worry. I don't want you around if you don't want our baby. You won't have to be 'a part of this,'" she replied harshly and turned to leave the kitchen. She couldn't bear to remain near Nick.

"Do you have the number for Bess?"

With her back to him, she said, "Yes, I marked it on the pad by the phone. G-give her my love."

Andrea returned to the bedroom and gathered up her belongings, furiously packing the small bag she'd brought with her. Then she stripped the bed of its linen, replacing it with clean sheets.

After straightening the bathroom, she went to the living room. The tray with her empty soup bowl remained on the coffee table, mocking her with memory of Nick's tender care. Until he found out the reason for her nausea.

The phone rang again, and Andrea fought the urge to rush to the kitchen. Nick would let her know when they could leave. After all, he wouldn't be anxious to remain any more than she was.

Just as she'd guessed, immediately after she heard him hang up the phone, he came into the living room. She looked at him, waiting for him to speak.

"My office can't find a helicopter around here to hire. They've all been pressed into duty by the local authorities because the dam broke."

"Oh, no!" Andrea knew there were a lot of farms in the low-lying valley just below the nearby dam. "No wonder they couldn't come get us."

"Yeah."

"What are we going to do?"

"My company helicopter is flying down from Chicago. But it'll take a few hours to make the trip, and they can't find us after dark. They'll come in first thing in the morning."

In the morning. Another night with Nick.

"I talked to Bess," he continued, "and she's okay.

The helicopter will pick her up before it comes to get us tomorrow.''

"She's going to stay here? I don't think—"

"Of course not. I told her she was coming back to Chicago with me until the flooding stops."

She wished she could insist that Bess stay with her in Kansas City. The elderly woman's calm good sense would come in handy. But she was Nick's aunt, not hers.

Loneliness swamped her. She had no one. Her hands crept to her stomach and she folded them across her. No, she wasn't alone. She had her child, and she must be strong for her child. She lifted her gaze to Nick to find him staring at her stomach.

"Are you sick every morning?" he asked abruptly.

"No. If I eat crackers and get up slowly afterward, I don't usually get sick."

"Crackers," he repeated flatly. "You were eating crackers the other morning."

"Yes."

"When were you going to tell me? Were you ever going to let me know about the baby?"

She couldn't believe the anger in his voice. How dare he get upset with her? He's the one who didn't want the baby. "What difference does it make to you? Wouldn't you be happier not knowing?"

"You think I'd prefer to believe you didn't love me?" The pain in his voice cooled her own anger.

Bowing her head, she gathered herself together. Best to simply answer his question. "I planned to tell you after the baby was born."

"But you were forced to tell me now. Too bad."

"I'd already changed my mind," she said sturdily, holding on to her temper. "I was going to tell you before you walked out."

He gave her a scornful look, as if he didn't believe her.

"I said I had something to tell you. I thought you should know before you left. In…in case I didn't see you again."

"Are you sure you're pregnant? Have you seen a doctor?"

"I'm not an idiot, Nick. Of course I've seen a doctor. I'm definitely pregnant. The baby's due in November."

"November?" he demanded harshly.

"Yes, near your birthd—" She made the connection between his reaction and the delivery date. Of course. All the more reason for Nick to believe everything would go wrong. "Nick, I'm fine. The baby is fine. Nothing bad is going to happen." She took a deep breath and then added, "Except my child won't know his father."

Nick gave a harsh laugh. "*Your child* might count that a plus." Without saying anything else, he left her alone.

They avoided each other the rest of the day. For supper, Andrea made sandwiches and left Nick's in the kitchen while she took hers to the living room. She'd managed to listen to a weather report and discovered that mild weather had returned. She would be sleeping on the couch tonight.

A little before ten, Nick opened the living room door. Andrea was curled up in the big chair, pretending to read by candlelight, but she had no idea what the book was about.

"I've heated your bathwater."

She was tempted to skip the bath and wait until tomorrow when she could take a hot shower, but she didn't. The hot water and the feel of cleanliness would help her sleep after a tense day. "Thank you." Nick reached out his hand for Noah, and she reluctantly handed her pet over to him so he could put him in the box in the kitchen.

Following Nick from the room, she entered the bedroom and unpacked the necessities. Then, once she was sure Nick was back in the kitchen, she took another quick bath. Not because of the cold, this time, but because she wanted to be done with their ordeal.

After she came out of the bath, she gathered together the sheet and covers, along with her pillow, to make up her bed on the couch.

"What are you doing?" Nick asked as he met her in the hallway.

"Fixing my bed."

"You're sleeping in the bed with me. It's stupid to be uncomfortable when we've shared the bed the past two nights." He tried to take the bedding from her.

She clung to the quilts as if they were her lifeline. "There's no need tonight. It's not going to be that cold."

"Andy, you need a good night's rest. Tomorrow is

going to be stressful. You've never flown in a helicopter, have you?''

She frowned. What difference did that make? "No, but—"

"You're going to have a long day. We'll both sleep in the big bed tonight. Do you need me to promise I won't touch you?"

Though she knew her body hadn't changed that much because of her pregnancy, the tone of his voice made her feel ugly and unattractive. "No," she whispered. "You don't need to promise." She turned loose of the bedding, except for her pillow, and headed back to the bedroom.

"Andy—"

She ignored him. Suddenly any discussion was beyond her. Crawling into the bed, she put her pillow back in its place and pulled the cover over her. Closing her eyes, she wished tomorrow was over.

"You forgot Noah," Nick said.

She opened her eyes to find him standing beside the bed, the puppy in his big hand. "Thank you. Could you get me a towel for him?"

"Sure."

He returned at once with a folded towel to make a pad for the puppy.

"Thank you."

"You're welcome."

How civil they'd become. Because they had nothing else to say to each other. She closed her eyes.

* * *

How could she have been so stupid? She'd forgotten her crackers. The next morning, she elbowed Nick, who was still asleep.

"Nick? I forgot my crackers. Could you get out of bed, carefully, and bring me some."

"Carefully?" he asked, shaking his head, as if to clear it.

"Don't...don't rock the bed."

"Oh." He slid from the bed with the minimum of motion and left the room.

Noah, wakened by Andrea's voice, crawled up to lick her face.

"Good morning, Noah," she whispered. "I don't think your kisses will help me." Nick's appearance cut short any more talk with the dog. "Thanks," she murmured as she took the crackers from him.

"Want me to help you sit up?"

"No, I have to stay flat while I eat the crackers."

He stood there, staring down at her, as she tried to calm her unruly stomach, making the task even more difficult than usual. Finally she eased into a sitting position, not making any sudden movement.

"That's all it takes? Some crackers?" Nick asked incredulously.

"Most of the time."

Before he could say anything else, the phone rang. He picked up the extension by the bed. "Hello? Yeah. Fifteen minutes. We'll be ready."

"Fifteen minutes until they get here?" she gasped, already getting out of bed.

"Yeah. But Bess will have to pack a few things,

so you don't have to be ready to leave quite that soon.''

She closed the bathroom door as he finished. There was no time to waste.

The sound of a helicopter landing near the house came almost exactly fifteen minutes later. She shouldn't have been surprised. Nick demanded the best of all those around him.

Andrea stood in the kitchen, her bag packed, the house straightened and ready for Bess's arrival. When the door opened and Nick's aunt came into sight, Andrea was suddenly overwhelmed with emotion. Ignoring Nick, who'd gone out to meet the helicopter, Andrea threw herself into Bess's waiting arms, tears spilling down her cheeks.

"Oh, Bess, I'm so glad you're all right," she exclaimed, trying to gulp back her tears.

"Here, now, child, of course I'm fine. How about you? Did you manage by yourselves?"

Bess's comforting arms held her and Andrea felt the warmth and acceptance Bess had always given her, along with her love. She wiped her eyes and tried to smile. "Yes. We used a lot of your groceries, but we're fine."

Blue eyes quite similar to Nick's studied her closely, and Andrea felt her cheeks flush. It was hard to hide anything from Bess.

Instead of asking her, Bess turned to Nick. "What's wrong?"

Andrea rushed to answer, not wanting Bess to worry. "Nothing, Bess."

At the same time, with grim harshness, Nick said, "She's pregnant."

Bess's eyes lit up and her face broke into a huge smile. Once more, she embraced Andrea, and, for the first time, Andrea was able to share her happiness and excitement over the baby. The two exchanged half sentences, each trying to answer questions and ask their own.

Nick put an end to the moment. "We need to go. Go pack, Bess."

After a look at her nephew's face, Bess turned to Andrea with understanding eyes and squeezed her hands. "It won't take but a minute. Why don't you get Andy settled in the helicopter?" She leaned forward to kiss Andrea's cheek. "Don't worry," she whispered. "He'll come around."

Chapter Twelve

As Andrea had feared, Bess was overly optimistic about her nephew's attitude.

The helicopter had flown them straight to Kansas City. She and Bess had sat in the back seats, Noah in Andrea's lap, leaving Nick and one of his assistants to take the front seats. Conversation had been impossible, but Bess had held Andrea's hand and given her delighted smiles all the way.

Nick had occasionally glared at them. The rest of the time he'd been on the telephone or conversing with the other men.

When they reached Kansas City, Andrea got off the helicopter with relief and thanked the pilot for coming to get them. Bess got out, too, and Andrea turned to hug her goodbye, shifting Noah to one side so he wouldn't be crushed.

"I'm going to miss you, Bess. Let me know when

you're coming home, and I'll drive down and get your house ready.''

"Don't be silly, child. Do you think I'm going to leave you alone now? You need company. I'm staying here with you and that dratted dog.''

Andrea's eyes widened and she looked at Bess with growing hope. "Would you, Bess? I promise I'll be strong enough to stay alone soon, but it would mean so much if you could—''

Bess grinned. "When have I ever passed up the opportunity to boss someone around? You're looking a little too piqued to please me. I'm going to take care of you, and we'll soon have you and junior in good shape.''

Nick came over to them. He'd gotten out of the helicopter first and gone into the nearby office. "Andrea, a car is picking you up. It should be here any minute. I've arranged for a new car to be delivered to your apartment first thing in the morning.''

"But, Nick, you shouldn't—''

He acted as if she'd never spoken. Turning to his aunt, he said, "Bess, we'd better be on our way. I'll help you into the helicopter.''

"I'm not going," Bess said calmly, smiling at her nephew as if she'd turned down the offer of a sandwich.

Frowning, he protested, "Bess, you can't go back to your house until the weather improves.''

"I'm not. I'm staying here in Kansas City with Andy. She needs some family support right now.'' Bess's facial expression never changed, but Andrea could sense the anger in Nick, as if his aunt had criticized his behavior.

He glared at both of them. When neither of them spoke, he muttered, "Fine. If you need anything, call."

Stepping into the helicopter, he didn't look back at either of them. The man standing nearby motioned to them to step back and they moved closer to the building where their bags had been set down. Bess waved as the helicopter lifted off from the ground, but there was no return wave.

When the noise had subsided and the helicopter was a mere speck in the sky, Andrea whispered, "I'm afraid he's very angry, Bess. He may not forgive you for staying here."

"Nonsense, Andy. I think he's still in shock. When did you tell him about the baby?"

"Not until yesterday."

"Well, that explains it, child. Men don't handle these situations well."

"But, Bess, he said he'd never have a child because…because of his father. That's why I left him. I want my baby to be loved."

"And it will be, Andy. I'll be the best grandmother any baby has ever had. And Nick will change his mind, you'll see."

Andrea had no doubts about Bess fulfilling her chosen role. But Nick was another matter.

Once they finally arrived at Andrea's modest apartment, Bess looked around surprised. "Is this the best Nick can afford?"

"Nick's not paying for my apartment, Bess. I am. I have to learn to stand on my own two feet."

"Humph!" Bess growled, sounding like her nephew.

That thought brought a range of emotions to Andrea. Already she missed Nick, though he'd only been gone an hour. And she had to face the fact that this time their separation was permanent.

"I'll put your things in the bedroom," Andrea said, and hurried into the other room.

"Where will you sleep?" Bess asked, following her.

"On the sofa."

"You'll do no such thing. Expectant mothers need good rest. I'll take the sofa."

Andrea smiled. "No, Bess. I won this argument with your nephew and I'll win with you, too. The sofa is fine for me."

"He let you sleep on the sofa at my house? I'm going to have to have a long conversation with my nephew," Bess promised, steely determination in her eyes.

"Bess, please don't try to persuade Nick to…to accept me and the baby." Andrea bit down on her bottom lip to keep it from trembling before she continued. "If…if he truly doesn't want our child, then I'd rather live alone…without him. I won't have my child become anyone's duty."

Bess's gaze saddened and she took both of

Andrea's hands in hers. "All right, child. I understand." Then she looked around the room. "But that
doesn't mean he shouldn't provide adequately for
you. My great-niece or nephew needs more room and
a yard and…and a happy mother. Nick may not be
able to handle being a father, but he can certainly be
a better provider."

"But, Bess, Nick—"

"Will do as his aunt tells him," Bess promised in
a voice that would withstand any arguments.

It began the next morning.

Promptly at eight o'clock, the doorbell pealed,
rousing Noah to a chorus of barks. When Andrea
opened the door, a gentleman dressed in a three-piece
suit introduced himself and asked her to accompany
him so he could show her her new car.

A Mercedes.

"Mr. Avery felt the safety features of this car
would protect you. You'll notice—"

She listened to him, but scarcely heard what he
said. Nick would, of course, not think about the cost
of a car. Or the insurance. She wasn't sure she could
afford the rise it would mean in her insurance rates.

When she returned to the apartment, two sets of
keys in her hands, Bess was just hanging up the
phone.

"Nice car?"

"Yes, it's beautiful. I need to call my insurance
agent, though. I don't want to drive it until it's properly insured."

"Nick's taken care of that," Bess assured her.

Surprised, she stared at Bess. "Oh. How nice. Um, I need to call work. I'm sure they think I've disappeared off the face of the earth." When she reached her office, her call was put through to her supervisor.

"Mrs. Campbell," Andrea said as soon as the lady answered. "I'm sorry. I was trapped in a farmhouse in Missouri because of the floods. The phone went out and I had no way to let you know what had happened."

"That's quite all right, Mrs. Avery."

Her use of Andrea's married name was the first clue that things had changed. Andrea had used her maiden name, Bainbridge, at work. "Avery? I don't—"

"Your husband called this morning to tell us what had happened, and also to give us your good news. Congratulations. Of course, we understand that you don't feel up to working your two weeks' notice. Mr. Avery assured us that you'd use our firm to decorate your new home."

When Andrea finished the conversation, sticking to generalities, she was seething. "Bess! Nick resigned my job *for me* this morning."

"Yes, he told me."

"But he has no right to do that! I have to support myself and my child."

Bess put her arm around Andrea's shoulders. "Andy, you're being silly. Nick has plenty of money, and it's his duty to take care of you."

"I told you, I didn't want to be anyone's *duty* ever again. Not me nor my child!"

She was trembling, fighting back tears, wanting so much more than a new car, freedom from work.

"Andy, he loves you," Bess whispered in her ear. "Give him time...and let him do what he can now."

The phone rang.

"Mrs. Avery? This is Dr. Lovelace's office. We understand you've just had a few traumatic days. Your husband thinks it would be a good idea if you came in for a checkup. Would tomorrow at ten be all right?"

The doorbell rang.

"Mrs. Avery? We have a delivery for you," the young man told her, his arms filled with a large cardboard box. "Your husband ordered groceries this morning."

The phone again.

"Mrs. Avery? I'm Ryan White with Kansas City Realty. Your husband wanted me to show you some property you might be interested in. Something with a large yard, plenty of space. Would this afternoon be all right?"

After a morning filled with Nick's good intentions, Andrea was exhausted. Bess fed her lunch and then tucked her into bed for a rest.

Left alone, without the constant barrage of people willing to serve her because of Nick's money, Andrea shed a few tears and was feeling sorry for herself. Why couldn't Nick understand that all the money in the world wouldn't give her what she needed most? Him.

She...and her baby...needed him to want them, to

spend time with them, to love them. Nothing could replace that priceless gift.

After a few minutes of self-indulgence, she pulled herself together. Too many women faced pregnancy alone without any of the luxuries Nick was showering upon her. She would be grateful for what he was giving her. It wouldn't replace him, but it would make her life easier.

And she had Bess.

She'd make it, her and her child. They'd build a new life. And hope and pray that Nick changed his mind.

A week later movers transported her meager belongings into the house Nick had purchased. It was roomy and spacious, elegant, and had a huge covered porch and backyard. Perfect for a child. And Noah.

And proof that Nick had no intention of being a part of their lives. After all, his work was in Chicago.

Her old decorating firm had already begun work to furnish the house. The first thing Andrea requested was a bed for the master bedroom. After a week on the sofa, she was ready for a good night's sleep. Though she wasn't sure it was the sofa that had had her tossing and turning.

With Bess around to organize everything, Andrea didn't have a lot to do. Nick seemed determined to leave her twiddling her thumbs. Someday soon, she'd have to determine what she was going to do. But right now, she didn't have the energy.

The sunroom, Andrea's favorite room in the new

house, was furnished first. The brightly flowered sofa trimmed in bamboo was flanked by chairs in primary colors that matched the colors in the flowers. A ceiling fan lazily stirred the air, as if an outdoor breeze was drifting through.

Plants enhanced the outdoor feeling, along with the huge windows that let in the sunshine. Here, Andrea felt a sense of peace, away from the hustle and bustle of the workmen who seemed to be constantly parading through the house.

"Here's a glass of lemonade and some muffins, Andy," Bess said, coming into the room.

"Bess, you don't have to wait on me," Andrea assured her, setting aside the furniture catalogs the decorator had left with her.

"These first three months are important. You need to get plenty of rest and nutrition. You still haven't gained any weight."

"Bess, you never had a child?"

She sat beside Andrea on the sofa. "I was pregnant once. But I lost him, a little boy, when I was three months. And I never conceived again."

"I'm so sorry," Andrea whispered, placing one hand on her stomach.

"It's all right. I had Nick. He was my son. Still is, in spite of his pigheadedness." Bess grasped Andrea's hand. "I thought he'd come around before now."

Andrea shook her head. "No. He made it clear how much he hates the idea of being a father."

"He's scared. That's not the same at all," Bess protested stoutly.

"The end results are the same. He's not here."

They sat silently, thinking about the stubborn man they both loved.

Finally, Bess asked, "Did you sleep any better last night, in your new bed?"

Andrea hadn't, but she wasn't going to worry Bess. "Yes, it was fine. It'll just take a little time to get used to it."

The doorbell rang, and Bess patted her hand as she stood. "I'll get that. You eat your muffins."

Andrea relaxed against the sofa cushions and sipped a little lemonade. Somehow she didn't have the appetite, even for one of Bess's muffins. She set down the glass of lemonade and closed her eyes. Maybe she'd rest a little.

"Have you been overdoing it?" a deep masculine voice asked.

Her eyes popped open and she stared at the one person she'd thought had disappeared from her life. "Nick!" As she tried to stand, he hurried to her side.

"Sit back down. You don't look any stronger than you did a week ago. Haven't you been resting?" His fierce gaze weakened her knees even more and she subsided against the cushions.

"What are you doing here?" she whispered, her gaze never leaving him as he sat beside her, taking her hand in his.

"I wanted to see how you were doing. If everything was satisfactory."

Of course. He was always thorough. He would want to know if his orders were being carried out. The flicker of hope that he had changed his mind swiftly died.

"Everything's fine. You've been very generous." She tried to infuse some gratitude in her voice, but it came out flat.

"You don't sound happy."

Irritation filled her. What did he want from her? "I'll write you a thank-you letter filled with gratitude and you can frame it. Okay?" She bit her lip in regret. With a sigh, she added, "Sorry, Nick. I'm a little short-tempered right now."

"Are you feeling all right?"

"Fine." *Other than missing you desperately. Feeling so lonely I could cry. Wanting your arms around me.*

He continued to stare at her, but she looked away.

"The car's working all right?"

"Fine."

"You like the house?"

"I love the house, Nick. Everything's fine. You've been more than generous." What else could she say? *You've given me all the wrong things.* She couldn't say that.

"How's Noah?"

"He's fine, too. He loves the backyard. He's out exploring right now."

Nick stood, and her gaze flew to his face. She thought she'd wanted him to leave, but now she couldn't stand the idea. But instead of walking to the door, he crossed the room to stare at the backyard, his hands in his pockets. "I've been thinking."

"Yes?"

"The baby won't be born for at least six more months."

"That's right." What now? Had he changed his mind about her not working?

"There's no reason for us to stay apart right now." He kept his back to her, so she couldn't see his face.

The meaning of his words sank in, and she stared at him in despair. "What are you saying?"

He whirled around, that fierce look in his eyes again. "I'm saying I want you, damn it! I miss you." Before Andrea could even think of moving, he was beside her on the couch again, pulling her into his embrace.

"Nick—" she began, but his lips covered hers, ending any remark she might have made. How heavenly to be wrapped in his arms again. To feel his lips on hers. But in spite of the overwhelming sensations that filled her, that was also a sadness.

She pulled away. "Don't, Nick." Standing, she walked several feet away from him.

"Why? I love you, Andy. You love me. At least, you said you did."

"You know I love you," she said tautly.

"Then why shouldn't I hold you? Make love to you?"

She blinked back tears and crossed her arms, trying to hold on to her self-control. "Because I can't face another goodbye in six months."

Expecting him to leave and not wanting to see him go, she turned her back. Nothing happened. He didn't move. She turned back around, to ask him why he was prolonging the agony. He was sitting on the couch, his face buried in his hands.

"Nick?"

From behind his hands, his muffled voice asked, "What if I promised not to go?"

She returned to the sofa and took his hands in hers, pulling them from his face.

"What did you say?"

"I asked what if I promised not to go?"

"Why, Nick?"

"I've already told you. I love you, Andy." His gaze remained fixed on their hands, joined together.

"We're not the only ones involved, Nick. Not any longer. There's a baby growing in me. A baby I love with all my heart. I want your love, but I will accept no less for my child. If you can't love our baby, then...then you can't stay."

He jerked his hands from hers and stood to stride across the room. She watched him, but said nothing.

Finally he whirled around to face her. "Damn it, Andy, I love the baby."

She said nothing, unsure he meant what he'd said.

Emotions seemed to be choking him. He looked away and said in a low voice, "I'm afraid."

She rose and crossed to his side. "Nick, I trust you. You could never be cruel to your child. You're not your father."

"But how can you be sure? How can you believe...believe everything will be all right?"

"I don't know that everything will be all right. But I know everything will be better if we're together. I know that we can face whatever life gives us with greater strength as two, than apart."

He pulled her against him, his strong arms wrapping around her. "I believe that, too," he whispered. "But I want to be a good father, and I'm afraid I can't."

"You can be," she assured him. "You're such a loving, giving man. If you love our baby, Nick, I'd trust you to be just as protective of it as you are of me."

"I'll protect the baby from anything, but what if I can't protect it from me?"

"I'll help you. You'll see."

"Are you sure?" he asked hoarsely.

"Oh, Nick," she replied, joy filling her watery chuckle, "you're going to be the best father in the world to all our children."

He kissed her but pulled away before Andrea wanted him to. "Wait a minute. All our children? You're not having twins, are you?"

"No. But you don't want our baby to be an only child, do you? Weren't you lonesome?"

"Yes, but—"

"Don't worry. You'll be a great daddy," she promised, her heart overflowing with happiness.

"How about if we take it one baby at a time?" he suggested shakily before his lips returned to hers.

Epilogue

Andrea scanned the entryway as she came down the stairs. Three years ago when she'd first moved into the big house, she'd been very conservative in her choice of decor.

Now she thought it was time to be more creative. Besides, she'd found the perfect piece of furniture, an antique table, to replace the tallboy gracing the hall now.

She'd have to ask Nick if he minded the change. He'd grown very sentimental over everything connected to the move.

"Nick, are you ready?" she called.

"Um, Andy? There's been a change of plans," he returned from the sunroom.

Andrea rolled her eyes. She knew what was coming. Walking briskly, she entered the back room. "A change of plans?"

"Daddy can't go," a little voice piped up, sending her mother a triumphant grin. "He's having tea with me and Noah."

Elizabeth Ann Avery, who would turn three in four more months, could twist her father around her little finger...and she knew it. Smiling adoringly at the handsome man who overpowered the child's table beside which he sat, she offered him another cookie from the plate in front of her. "Please try another of Aunt Bess's cookies, Daddy."

"Really, Nick, you promised you'd go," Andrea reminded her husband.

"That's true. And if you want, I will go with you. But Bess mentioned an interest in going, and I thought I'd stay with Betsy." An identical smile to her daughter's tried to charm the right answer out of her.

She stared at the two of them, her hands on her hips. "It's not fair to gang up on me," she protested.

"You can stay for tea, too, Mommy," Betsy generously offered, patting the back of the small chair next to her.

"Thank you, sweetheart, but I really need to go to this sale. I've seen several things that would do well in my shop."

Once she and Nick had gotten back together, they'd decided to remain in Kansas City, with Nick making only occasional trips to Chicago. He worked at home by computer most of the time. Andrea had begun searching for furnishings for their home. Somehow, her searches had resulted in a huge inventory. It had seemed reasonable to open a small shop.

Now one of the must-sees for decorators and their clients, the shop threatened to take over her life. Especially since she'd been slowing down the last eight months.

"All right, you two, I give. You can stay with Betsy, Nick. And there's no need to bother Bess. I can manage on my own."

"No way," Nick said firmly, rising to cross the room and loop his arms around her. "You're not going out on your own. It's too close to time."

"I should hope it's close to time. If I get much bigger, you won't be able to put your arms around me," she fussed, staring at her enlarged belly. "I feel like a beach ball with legs."

"But you're the most beautiful beach ball I've ever seen," he teased, kissing her.

"Kiss me, too, Daddy!" Betsy insisted, tugging on her father's pantleg. Noah, who had remained at Betsy's side the entire time, followed her and gave a patient bark. He was devoted to their child.

"Of course, my sweet," Nick agreed with a laugh, swinging his little daughter high in the air before planting a big kiss on her cheek.

Betsy hugged his neck. "You're the bestest daddy ever," she squealed.

Nick glowed at her praise, and his gaze met Andrea's. "Thanks to your mommy, little one."

"Oh, no, Nick," Andrea returned, smiling at her husband. "You didn't need any help. From the moment you held Betsy in your arms, you were caught, hook, line and sinker.''

He laid his palm on her stomach. ''Think it will be the same with the next one?''

''Probably even worse,'' she whispered before kissing him again.

''I'm ready to go,'' Bess called as she entered the sunroom.

''Auntie Bess, Daddy's having tea with me,'' Betsy announced.

''My, what a surprise. What does that make, the third tea party this week? And it's only Thursday.'' Bess grinned at Nick and Andrea.

''We'd best be on our way, Bess, if you're sure you want to come.''

''I wouldn't miss it for the world, Andy. I think we should look for some more teapots. They've been doing real well at the shop.''

With quick goodbyes, the two women headed for Andrea's car. After they settled in, Bess said, ''See, I told you he'd come around.''

''Yes, you did. He's the best daddy in the world. And an even better husband.''

''Yep, he learned his lesson in the *Nick* of time,'' Bess crowed, joking as she had the past three years.

But for Andrea, it was a truth she held dear to her heart. Nick had come around to loving her *and* their baby just in time for all of them.

* * * * *

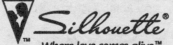

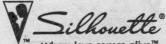